NEVER LOVE
A HOSER

piwi

ISBN-13: 978-1-928076-14-8
ISBN-10: 1928076149

ii

THIS BOOK IS DEDICATED TO D.H.,
WHO WAS *SUCH* A GOOF

What happened before

Mrs. Calestini stirred and tasted the soup. It was hot, rich and thick, just the way it was supposed to be. She smiled, telling herself for the hundredth time that she was the best damned cook around. She let the soup simmer as she began making ravioli stuffed with chicken. She sighed, grateful for the cool, breezy June day that was now turning into a dark, chilly evening. She had trouble coping with hot weather and enjoyed living in Vancouver, a rainy, gray city. She turned on the kitchen light and continued working.

These Canadian girls, she said to herself. *They make sure that they don't have to go through pregnancy in the summer! They actually plan their pregnancies! Whoever heard of such foolishness? In the old country, you just did what came naturally. If you were meant to have babies, you had them.* She had a right to think that Canadian girls were fools.

She was a midwife and business had been slow all summer. She also had seven children of her own to feed since her husband had dropped dead.

Just then the doorbell rang with a loud round clang. She frowned, trying to think of who it might be. Probably a door-to-door salesman; they got enough of those people in her neighborhood. "Gina," she called out, "go see who's at the door." Her voice sounded old and nasty from all the yelling she'd had to do over the years.

Gina didn't reply, and when the doorbell rang again, the woman wiped her hands and marched down the hallway. She opened the door and saw a young woman standing there, obviously pregnant. Due any day, Mrs. Calestini told herself.

"Are you the midwife?" asked the girl, swallowing hard.

"Yes, I am." She could tell right away that this one was a lady. She spoke carefully and held herself erectly. Her parents had raised her well, taught her some manners.

The girl swallowed again. "I'm very sorry to bother you but I'm new in Vancouver and have nowhere else to go."

Mrs. Calestini frowned. If she took the girl in, Noelle would have to give up her bedroom, and Gina wouldn't like that. Gina hated to sleep with her sisters. Maybe this new woman didn't have any money. Maybe she wasn't even married. But then she noticed a small diamond ring on the girl's finger.

"In case you're wondering," the young lady said, "I have some money."

"But I don't have any room," Mrs. Calestini replied.

"Please make room for me." The girl breathed hard. "I have nowhere else to go. I'll sleep on the floor…"

Mrs. Calestini nodded. "Come in." If Gina didn't like sleeping with her sisters, too bad.

The young woman followed the older woman down the hallway and up one flight of stairs. When they reached Gina's room Mrs. Calestini turned on the light. She could see the girl's face brighten with pleasure.

"Take off your jacket," said Mrs. Calestini. "Sit down and be comfortable." Then, "How long ago did the pains start to come?"

"About an hour ago. I wanted to keep walking but it was impossible. That's why I'm here." She added, "This wasn't how I wanted to have my baby. I wanted to be in a hospital with Andy by my side."

Mrs. Calestini saw that the girl was petite; the birth might be difficult. Still, the older woman felt delighted by the prospect of another girl becoming a woman as a result of becoming a mother. This birth might have complications, but the midwife said nothing. She smiled. "You will become a mother soon. It is one of nature's finest gifts. I know; I have been gifted seven such times myself."

The girl smiled. "Thank you for your good wishes."

"Climb into bed and try to sleep. I will come up again soon and see how you are feeling." As she left, she realized she had not asked the girl's name. *Well, she thought, I'll ask her in a few hours. I hope she can sleep, but I doubt she will.*

The girl crawled into bed and did her best to sleep but could not. All she could think about was Andy and their home. *I wonder what they think of me*

It had been raining hard and the wind had nearly knocked her off her feet as she left their apartment to meet him by the restaurant. She had waited for two hours before going back home. She telephoned his office and they told her he had gone home for the night. He had disappeared; she had no idea where he was. He was hardly the type of man who would just go off and get lost. She felt convinced that something tragic had happened to him.

She lay in bed and stared out the window. So this was Vancouver, one of Canada's largest cities and one of its rainiest, too. The thing to remember was that in this city it rained every other day throughout the year. If you liked that sort of weather—as apparently many people did—then Vancouver was an easy place to fall in love with. She wondered how easy it would be to keep your spirits up when the weather was so dreary so often. She closed her eyes and listened to the kitchen sounds downstairs.

When the children clambered in for dinner, Mrs. Calestini shushed them right away, saying that there was someone new upstairs. When Gina protested losing her room because of a new person, Mrs. Calestini promised her a reward if she put up with the inconvenience for the next little while.

Presently the woman went upstairs and said to the girl, "How do you feel?"

The girl shrugged. "All right, I suppose."

"How often are the pains coming?"

"Every half hour."

"That's good," Mrs. Calestini lied. There was hardly any dilation at all. She went downstairs and told the other girls that a new baby was due at any time.

At just before midnight a big storm filled the Vancouver sky with thunder, lightning and torrential rain. Just after midnight the baby was born. Its mother just lay there, her face taut and sweaty with terror. Mrs. Calestini told her oldest son to go around the corner and get Dr. Waldman. Then she added that he should get a priest, too.

The doctor delivered the baby and slapped its buttocks. It began to wail, no doubt partly over being pulled out of its war, wet womb. Mrs. Calestini watched with hand-wringing anxiety as the doctor did his best to save the young mother's life. The older woman knew that the doctor's best wasn't good enough when he asked the priest to take over. As the priest stood over the girl Mrs. Calestini knelt by the bed and prayed.

She was amazed at how young and brave the girl was.

The older woman, too, had been young and brave once.

The girl turned her head and offered the woman a weak little smile that told the woman that the new mother knew her minutes were numbered. Mrs. Calestini put the newborn baby by its mother's head. The girl closed her eyes.

"You didn't tell me your name," said Mrs. Calestini.

"Frannie Stone." She kept her eyes closed and did not speak again.

"She's gone," murmured the doctor. "Now we'll fill out the birth certificate."

Mrs. Calestini nodded.

"What is the baby's name?"

"Francis Stone." Mrs. Calestini smiled. At least

the child now had a name, his mother's final gift to her son.

PART ONE

Chapter 1

Across the busy Vancouver street, high in the steeple of St. Anthony's, the bell began to chime for the eight o'clock Mass. The kids all stood in line waiting to go in and the sisters had just entered the yard. A moment earlier we had all scrambled around, teasing and yelling at each other, but now we stood rigid and orderly. We formed two rows and marched into the school as if we had just joined the Canadian Armed Forces. Presently we entered our classrooms and sat in silence.

"We will begin our day with a prayer," said Sister Theresa, as she did five mornings per week. We bent our heads and clasped our hands together.

"Francis," said Sister Theresa.

"Yes, ma'am?" Then, "I didn't do anything wrong."

"I didn't say you did. Please stand up and write today's date on the blackboard."

"Oh, O.K." I did as told and wrote *Friday, June 6, 1928.*

"Thank you, Francis," she said. "Please sit down."

The morning passed by and I felt bored. The air was warm and getting even warmer and school would be out soon. I had very little use for school. I was thirteen, a big mischievous boy, and my pal Clark would let me do his errands and collect his bets from the guys at the local hangouts. Clark let me do such errands because they were too trivial to interest him. I could make a dozen dollars per week, and that was a huge amount of money to me. Plus, I didn't give a *crap* about school.

At noon, the other kids went home to eat lunch. I would go to the dormitory building behind the school and have a sandwich, glass of milk and donut for lunch. It tasted good on most days and I probably ate better than most of the kids who went home for lunch. At one, we would go back to school for classes till three. I always felt like ditching. Damn, it was hot! I wanted to strip naked and go swimming. But I remembered what happened the last time I ditched school.

I think I set the world's record for truancy. I stayed away from school for six consecutive weeks. That is remarkable because I lived in the school and slept there every night. I would steal the written complaints about my ditching before Brother Lawrence read them. I forged replies saying that I was too sick for school. By and by they caught on to me; after a strenuous day watching four movies at the Capitol Theatre, I headed back and found Brother Lawrence and some sisters waiting for me. He demanded to know where I had been, with whom and what we had been up to. As I opened my mouth to spout forth some lies, he slapped me across the face.

Sister Theresa scowled. "Francis, how could you do this to us? You're supposed to be one of our best boys—the one who would go into the world and do great things. But instead you're off doing your own thing instead of going to school and getting an education!"

If all else fails, I'd always told myself, try telling the truth. "I'm so sick of all this! Sick of you, sick of the school, sick of the orphanage! I'm just a prisoner here—people in Oakalla Prison have as much freedom as I do! I didn't do anything to be locked up for; I don't deserve any of this. You teach us that the Lord should be thanked for all He has given us. Well, what has *He* given *me*? My life is awful."

Sister Theresa's chin quivered—I thought she might start crying. Brother Lawrence pouted in a poor-baby kind of way. Sister Theresa said, "Francis, you said your life is awful, but you're very young yet and you have a chance for a better life if you study hard and attend school each day. Running around town and goofing off is the worst thing you can do. Don't ever do anything like that again. Understand?"

I nodded.

"All right, then. Brother Lawrence, Francis has promised to better from now on. We must give him an opportunity to show us that he means what he says. I will now go pray to God to forgive this boy." She walked away.

Brother Lawrence said, "Francis, you must be hungry. Go eat some supper."

At thirteen, I was a big boy, and a streetwise one, too. I would stop ditching that afternoon, no matter how much fun I could have, and I would go to school and be a colossal pain in Sister's butt.

At the schoolyard a baseball game was happening. My pal Clark sat and watched it with me. He and I were the best of friends. Sometimes I thought he was my only true friend in the world.

Chapter 2

I had lived at the orphanage that it really was the only home I had ever known. If I had missed out on family love and belonging, well, I didn't miss what I'd never had. If I didn't feel that the other kids at the orphanage were my family, I certainly thought of them as my friends who respected me. As a big boy, I had plenty of self-assurance and I also had street wisdom and charisma that most people do not acquire until they are much older.

I often had part-time employment and lent nickels and dimes to other kids who were better off than I was. I knew when they got their allowances and they knew better than to try not to repay me. A couple of weeks earlier I had lent a quarter to Pete Costa. When repayment day arrived, he eluded me but I caught up with him soon enough. He said he was broke, so I laid off for a week. But then I confronted him again.

"Hey, Pere," I said. "I want my money."

Pete thought he was a tough guy. He stood an inch or so shorter than I did but outweighed me by ten pounds or more. "Your money? What money?"

"My money that I lent you. I lent it to you, I didn't *give* it to you."

"Fuck you and your money too." He turned to his pals. "See, that's the trouble with those bastards who live at the orphanage. We feed them and clothe them and educate them and they have no gratitude. Well, he'll get his bloody money when I'm damn good and ready to pay it back."

I got mad. I didn't especially mind being called a bastard because that word had long since lost its power to offend me. Also, Brother Lawrence had often said, "You children are the luckiest because your only father is God Himself. That makes you truly blessed." No, being called a bastard didn't really faze me but having one of my borrowers hold out on me made me go bananas.

I pounced on him. He punched me on the chin and I collapsed. "You dago asshole!" I yelled. Incensed, he hauled off and punched me again. I could feel my nose bleed and drew up my knee. I kicked him in the scrotum and he went down with a tiny cry. He covered up his testicles as I lay into him. I kicked and punched him and all he could do was cry out and keep his hands over his privates.

I got up and dug my hand into his hip pocket. I counted out the money he owed me and said to his assembled friends, "You see this? I'm just taking what's mine, nothing more. If you borrow from me, you better pay me back or live with the consequences." They watched me walk away. There were three of them standing over their pal, and they could easily have jumped me, but they didn't.

I walked over to Tommy Stelfox's poolroom. Tom stood behind the cash register. He laughed when he saw me. "What happened, Francis? Get into a fight?"

I nodded. "Some guy decided he didn't want to settle up with me, so I had to give him a crash course in business ethics."

"Good for you. Your borrowers need to know at all times that they do not have the option to defaulting on their loans. You better get your nose cleaned up and then sweep the floor."

I nodded. The washroom reeked of urine and stale tobacco. I climbed onto the sink and opened the window above, letting a blast of warm June Vancouver air into the smelly room. I cleaned myself off and went back into the main room to start my shift.

My afternoons at Tommy's pool hall were the most fun I had. I would sweep the floor and clean up the pool tables. I wiped the table tops with the utmost care so I wouldn't damage the felt, then I'd polish the wood. Finally I would ice down the pop and beer; since Prohibition happened here just as in the States, we kept the beer downstairs and the patron who wanted it had to ask Tommy personally, and if Tommy was too busy to fetch it he would send me down for it.

At just after four o'clock the race results from Exhibition Park would come in and we would get ready. I would mark them down on a blackboard in an isolated part of the pool hall so that you had to know where to look in order to find it. I would rack the balls and run errands for the customers. Often I would hurry across the street to the delicatessen to get them sandwiches. I kept my shoeshine box in the poolroom in case anyone needed his skates glazed.

I used to make about three dollars per week plus whatever other action I could hustle up. Sometimes a man would say, "Kid, do you know where I could get a woman?" If I did, as was usually the case, I would send him to her and pocket a commission. As soon as summer vacation started Tommy was going to send me out each day to collect the small bets. He said I might make up to fifteen dollars per week at it. Later each afternoon Mr. Stelfox would give me all his betting slips to add up. Those slips contained all the action and I had to calculate the totals because Tom said it gave him a headache. At seven o'clock I would run back to the orphanage for dinner. Then I would go back for a couple of hours, but Mr. Stelfox said that Vancouver was a more dangerous neighborhood than most people thought and he sent me back to the orphanage well before midnight. I resented him a bit for considering me a child who couldn't look after himself.

Peter Costa did not attend school the next day,

but his mum did. She stood there scowling at me in front of everyone as she spoke to Sister Theresa, who sent her to Sister Superior. Presently a girl entered the classroom with a message for Sister Theresa.

"Mary Acheson will read the lesson during my absence," said Sister Theresa. "Francis, please come with me."

Off we went. We ended up in the Sister Superior's office, where Brother Lawrence stood talking to Mrs. Costa and the Sister Superior. Mrs. Costa was saying, "Unless you discipline these little troublemakers..." She stopped when she saw me enter the room.

The Sister Superior said, "Come here, Francis."

I did as told.

"They tell me that you got into a fight with Peter and hurt him badly. Why did you do that?"

I shrugged. "He owed me money but wouldn't pay up. Also, he called me a nasty name."

"Francis, you must learn to control your temper. Name-calling is harmless and Jesus instructs us all to ignore that sort of behavior. I want you to apologize to Mrs. Costa and tell her you won't harm Peter again."

I nodded. An apology was no big deal to me; it was just a bunch of air that cost me nothing. I said to Mrs. Costa, "I'm sorry about the fight. I didn't want to do it."

The Sister Superior said, "Francis, as punishment for fighting, I'm making to stay on school grounds after school for two weeks."

I shook my head. "No! You can't do that!"

"You're tellin' us what we can and cannot do, eh?" asked Brother Lawrence.

"If you punish me that way, someone else will get my job at Tommy Stelfox's pool hall."

"Oh, you have a job now, eh?" said Brother Lawrence. "Please tell us what you do over there."

"Honest work," I said. "Sweeping and cleaning and running errands."

"Well, we have enough of that kind of work here to keep you busy."

"Francis, you should go back to class now," said the Sister Superior.

"Let's go," said Sister Theresa. We left the room together and walked down the hallway. She stopped and grabbed my hand. "Don't feel low," she said. "Everything will be all right. Things have a way of sorting themselves out."

"You're very kind," I said. "You understand me. You care."

"You poor child," she said. In silence we walked towards the classroom.

Chapter 3

Avoiding Brother Lawrence became a very easy thing to do. I would just open a window, climb through it, take care of my business and get back in time to report to Brother Lawrence.

On one such day I met Aldo Chies.

Aldo Chies was the Number One Man in our neighborhood. He ran everything worth running: booze, gambling and, some said, even the heroin and prostitution rackets, which were insanely lucrative. He was the most respected—or at least feared—man in that part of Vancouver. Whenever he stopped by at Stelfox's, which was often, I would see him for a moment. He always brought his goons with him. Aldo Chies was tough, hard and smart. He didn't take bullshit from anyone. He didn't have to. I admired him enormously.

Sometimes, after a day of working at Stelfox's, I

would take my shoeshine box and head over to the speakeasies to make some extra money. On one particular afternoon I went to the speak at the corner of Granville and Davie. The speaks were the best places to make money.

I simply went from one customer to the next and said, "Like a shoeshine, sir?" It never hurt to be polite.

The fat, nasty bartender would glower at me. "Get out of here, kid. Don't you know that this place is for adults only?"

As I started towards the exit, some jerk stuck out his foot and tripped me. my shoeshine box fell from my shoulder and my glass bottles of polish broke on the tile floor, making a big ugly puddle. I sat there and looked down at the mess, wondering what to do about it.

I felt myself being pulled to my feet by the barkeep. He literally shook me as he shouted, "Get out! Get out! Get out!"

"I need my shine box!" I yelled.

"Get out!"

I broke free of his grasp and started stuffing my

brushes into my box. The bartender slapped me upside my head. "Take off, eh!"

"Let him go, Walter. I want a shine." The calm, deep voice came from just beyond us.

Walter looked up; I looked at Walter, whose face was dead-white and whose features looked pinched with fear and worry. The man who'd spoken was lean and handsome, in his mid-thirties. He wore a gray suit and his hat had a sharp brim. His black shoes gleamed; he certainly didn't need a shine. Aldo Chies to the rescue.

"O.K., Mr. Chies. Whatever you say." Walter stood up and wiped some sweat from his brow. He went back to behind the bar.

I went over to Aldo Chies' booth. With him sat a well-dressed young man and a pretty woman. "Thanks, Mr. Chies. But I'm afraid I can't give you a shine."

"Oh? Why not?"

"Because I spilled my stuff all over the floor."

He took out his wallet and withdrew a five-dollar bill. He handed it to me. "Go get what you need and come back so I can get my shoeshine."

I looked at that bill and swallowed hard. Damn! When had I ever received *paper* money for my own? I headed for the door as a porter started mopping up my mess. I overheard Chies' friend say, "Aldo, I'll bet you'll never get that shoeshine you've just overpaid for."

He laughed. "Yeah, I'll take that bet."

"That boy had probably never seen that much money in his life," said Aldo's female friend.

When I got back with the shoe polish Aldo and his friends were eating. At first I wanted to think that the five he had given me was mine forever, but then I thought better of it and gave him the change.

Then I knelt and shined his shoes.

Aldo's friend took out his wallet and handed some cash to him. "Never bet with Aldo Chies," the man said. "You'll always lose."

"Always." Aldo put the money away and laughed. To me he said, "What's your name, boy?"

"Francis Stone, sir. Sometimes my friends call me Frank."

"Oh, are we friends now? You should choose your friends more carefully than that." Aldo and his friends laughed.

I frowned. "I don't know what you mean. I know all about you. I think you're great."

Aldo's two friends stood up. "Got to go now, Aldo. See you next time."

After they were gone, I said, "Mr. Chies, I want you to know that I won't be shining shoes forever. I want to do big things in Vancouver. I'm no fool. I know what's goin' on."

"That right, eh? Sit down and have a sandwich."

I nodded and sat across from him.

"Where do you come from?" he asked me.

"I live at the orphanage."

"So I guess you know the world a bit better than most of the other boys your age."

"I guess."

"Seems to me I've seen you before. Do you hang out at the playshops?"

The playshops were stores in our neighborhood that he had converted into little play areas for children. Everyone agreed that Aldo Chies was a big-hearted man to open those playshops for the benefit of the kids. I had overheard Stelfox say that those playshops were much more in Chies's self-interest than anyone realized. The playshops were full of fun machines that kids got to play for free; those same machines cost money for adults to play in bars and other places. Once the kids grew up, they were forbidden to enter the playshops; by then, they had become so fond of the fun machines that they spent too much money playing them in the other places. Aldo Chies always had his own interests in mind even when he *seemed* to be performing an act of altruism.

"I work at Tommy Stelfox's pool hall," I told him.

Aldo signaled over to the waiter, who hurried over to us. I ordered a pastrami sandwich and a glass of beer.

"You're a little young for beer," said Aldo. "You can have a pop instead."

The waiter brought me my sandwich and pop and I finished it in two minute. I was always hungry. "Thank you for that," I said.

He smiled. "You're welcome." Then, "Believe it or not, I was a shine boy just like you years ago." He reached into his pocket and gave me a few more bills.

"Take these. You never know when you'll need them."

"Thank you so much." I knew that these underworld guys, like everyone else in the world, liked it when the people they were generous to remembered to thank them. I smiled and walked out of the speakeasy.

At the street corner I encountered Cal Raymond, another shoeshine boy. I liked Cal; he was a friendly, decent kid. His father was an alcoholic; his family received welfare. Cal would turn over his earnings to his mum, who as often as not would buy hooch for the old man.

"Hey, Francis!" he said.

"Cal! How's it goin', eh?"

"Business is bad. Not making much money."

I flashed my five-dollar bill at him. His eyes nearly popped out of his skull. "Wow! Who'd you rob?"

"Didn't rob anyone. You just have to know the right people." I told him the truth about how I got the money.

"Aren't you the lucky one!" he exclaimed.

We walked down the street together. The sky

began to get dark. I wondered if it would rain again. It always seemed to rain in Vancouver.

"Mind coming upstairs with me?" he asked.

"Let's do it." I knew he wanted me to go inside with him because if he went in alone his mum or dad would hit him for not making any money.

We heard his mum and dad screaming at each other as soon as we got inside.

"Home sweet home," Cal muttered.

We started up the stairs. At the first landing a man came out of a room, hurried past us and went down the stairs. He left the door slightly open, and a voice from within called out, "Is that you, Cal?"

Cal stopped and said, "Yeah." To me he said, "That's Cass Merridy—I sometimes go to the store for her."

She came to the door and said, "I need you to go to the deli and get me a few bottles of beer. How about it?"

He nodded. "Yeah, Cass." He lay his shoeshine kit on the door, accepted the change from her outstretched hand and hurried off.

She said to me, "You don't have to wait there all

by yourself. Bring your boxes and come in."

I nodded and did as told.

Cass said, "See that chair? Have a seat."

Again, I did as told. I took a look at her; she was fairly tall and had blonde hair. I knew she was a prostitute. Vancouver had lots of working girls. I was a horny boy who was waiting for sexual opportunities. I wondered how much she would charge and what she would do for that price.

"I have some money," I told her.

"How nice for you," she retorted, snarling.

"Want some company?" I asked, smirking.

"Aren't you a little young?"

"I'm fifteen."

"You don't need to buy a girl—"

Just then Cal returned. "I got your beer, Cass."

I looked at her. She sat there checking me out, liking what she saw. I picked up my shine box and went down the hallway.

Cal said something and the woman laughed. Then they came to the door and she gave him a dime for running her errand. She started closing the door, then opened it wide, tossed a dime at me and said, "Cal there's a dime for your friend who was kind enough to wait for you."

I picked the dime off the floor and threw it at her. "Keep your dime, you bloody whore!" I ran out of that house as fast as I could.

Chapter 2

In just two weeks school would be over. Wonderful! I had no use for school; what I wanted was to spend my days at Tommy Stelfox's, where I could make real money.

I walked out of there with Steve. He said, "Francis, I thought you had to stay on the school grounds."

"My punishment is over."

"Got anything fun in mind for this afternoon?"

I shrugged. "Make me an offer."

"Francis, you want to go out into the country with me this summer?"

"Why would I want to do that?"

"Might be fun. I asked my dad and he said I should invite you over for dinner so we could talk about it."

"Your parents don't like me. Anyway, the idiots at the orphanage wouldn't let me go with you."

"They would if my dad said, 'Let the boy go.'"

Steve's father, of course, was Chip Rutledge, the mayor of Vancouver. We saw pictures of him every day—a handsome smiling man in a fine suit, teeth gleaming, everything's gonna be O.K. Chip Rutledge could get whatever he wanted from whomever he wanted it.

Soon we stood at the door of Stelfox's poolroom. Its interior was dim so I couldn't see inside very well. I thought of how I would feel about spending my summer in there, with all that bootleg beer and those toilets that practically overflowed with piss. Then I pictured spending the summer in the country with Steve. Maybe he had a big fancy place out that way with a swimming pool and servants and all kinds of fun stuff. There probably also was a lake I could swim in. That would be terrific; a couple of guys I knew who had been swimming in a lake told me it was way too much fun. Could be they were right. I turned to Clark and said, "Thanks but no thanks. I need to work this summer and make some money. Anyway, I hate the country. I'm a city boy."

Clark looked at me and guffawed. He was no

dummy; he knew why I wanted to stay in Vancouver. Clark wasn't an easy kid to make friends with, but he wasn't stuck-up, either. He was just—different. I didn't know why he liked me, but we sure hung out a lot together and I kept reminding myself that he was a valuable person to have in my life.

He shrugged. "O.K., have it your way. But I still want you to come over for dinner.

"I'll be there." We stood looking at each other for a moment. I said, "Well, I need to go to work now. Goodbye." He walked away and disappeared down the street.

I went into the poolroom and looked at the wall clock. It said the time was just after three; I was early. I didn't have to begin working till four, and at that moment I didn't feel like working at all. I looked around for Tommy and spotted him talking to some old fart I didn't know, so I skedaddled out of there and went up the street to the front steps of a huge stone apartment building and just sat there for the longest time, feeling wonderfully lazy. I thought of going to the country with Steve.

I smoked a cigarette and wished four o'clock

would never arrive when I heard shouting from across the street. Some of the local kids were bullying a Jewish boy. I felt way too lazy to go over and join in, so I smoked my cigarette and watched them have their fun. They stood in a half-circle as they snarled and yelled at him.

"Hey, Jewboy! Hey, kike!"

"How come you're so ugly? How come all Jews are so money-hungry? How come you have such big noses?"

The Jew stood there and snarled back at them. They inched their way towards him, their fists clenched. He put down his book and squared off, ready to fight. He was a decent-sized kid, a bit smaller than I. He had blond hair and blue eyes.

"I can take any of you in two minutes if it's one on one," he said matter-of-factly. Badly outnumbered though he was, he showed no fear.

The boys tormenting him burst out laughing. "Maybe you could," one of them said. "But we like the odds just the way they are."

I got up and bounded across the street. This was just too good to stay away from.

"Hey, Francis," one of the boys said.

"Hey, Wil," I replied.

"Let's kill this kike!" shouted another of the boys.

"No," I said. "He said he could take any of us one on one. You're not going to let him get away with speaking to you that way, are you? Well, he's going to fight one of us right now, so we have to figure out right now which one."

The boys frowned at me. I knew—and maybe they did, too—that they were all cowards except when they ganged up on someone. That Jew was a reasonably big kid who was ready to fight. Those bullies were not at all eager to mix it up with him.

"Time to fight," I said, shrugging. "Who's gonna punch him out?"

They all stared at the ground. Nobody said anything.

"I'll do it," I said.

I walked past them, towards the Jew. He kept his guard up, checking me out, asking himself if he could beat me in the fistfight that was about to happen.

I raised my fists. He stepped toward and threw a lame, wild punch at me. I ducked it with ease and stepped back. This boy was fairly big but he had no idea how to fight and he had no desire at all to hurt me or anyone else.

The boys cheered me on.

"Punch him out! Kick his ass!"

I backed up till I stood at the curb. Then I realized I still had my cigarette in my mouth, and I kept it there to show the Jew that I was a big tough dude who was not to be messed with. The Jew came up and swung at me a couple of times. I stepped away and all he punched was air. His strength seemed to fade quickly. I thought, *Wow! He knows I can take him, so why doesn't he just call it quits and run home?*

But he wouldn't go away, so I pounded him in the stomach and delivered a right cross to the chin. He went down and looked up at me.

"Beat his ass! Beat his ass!" the boys called out.

I shook my head. "Fight's over."

They looked at me, saw that I meant what I'd said, and then looked at the Jew. He stayed where he was, probably afraid that if he got up I would knock him back down.

I said to the bullies, "O.K., you've had your

46

entertainment for the day. You watched me kick his Jewish ass. Now go home."

The boys shrugged and wandered off. As soon as they were out of sight I took out my Players Lights and offered the Jew one. "Smoke?"

He shook his head. "Thanks for what you did."

I laughed. "You're thanking me for punching you out? That's a new one."

"Those punks...they wanted you to beat the shit out of me. You let me off easy. You didn't have to do that."

"Those boys weren't as mean as you think. If they were that mean, they would have pounded you themselves."

"They seemed mean enough to me," the Jew said as he got up and dusted off his book.

I eyed him as I blew out a stream of cigarette smoke. "You can't fight for shit. You better learn to defend yourself if you're going to live in this part of Vancouver, guy."

He snarled at me, and I could tell that he knew I was right. Vancouver had its share of bad dudes and tough guys and bullies, just like all other cities.

At that moment Father Slovick came down the street and I straightened up.

"Hello, Francis," he said.

"Good afternoon, Father," I replied.

"You haven't been fighting this boy, I hope." Father Slovick frowned at the kid.

Before I could speak, the Jew said to the priest, "Oh, no, sir. He was just teaching me some self-defense."

"Well, I just hope it was a lesson given to you for your own benefit. As you can see, Francis is a big boy who sometimes thinks that the best way to resolve a conflict is with his fists." Then, "What's your name, anyway? I can't ever recall seeing you at Mass."

"I'm Jewish. My name is Amnon Licthmann."

The priest nodded. "You must be Yoshe Lichtmann's son."

"Yessir, that's me."

The priest nodded. "Well, boys, you have a nice day and remember that fighting doesn't resolve anything. Goodbye."

He walked off, and the Jewboy said, "Well, he seems like a decent enough guy."

"He's all right...for a Catholic priest."

We walked down the street together. "Do you live around here?" I asked him.

"I live in Point Grey. My father owns the Canada Drugs chain."

"Nice for him." I looked into a store window and saw a clock that said it was just after four.

"I'm late for work. Gotta run."

"When your shift is over come over to my dad's store and I'll buy you a pop."

"Maybe I'll do that." I started to run; if I was too late, Stelfox would dock me.

Chapter 5

When I got there, Stelfox's was empty. It appeared that business was nonexistent that afternoon. I cleaned up the place right away, then did the arithmetic on his betting sheets and added the new numbers as the results came in.

After five o'clock, some customers came in to see about their bets. Tom sent me downstairs to get some bottles of ice-cold beer; when I got back upstairs, I saw Aldo Chies talking to my boss. He said, "Hello, Francis."

"Hello, Mr. Chies," I replied, delighted to be acknowledged by the Man.

He resumed speaking to Stelfox for a few more minutes, then said to me, "How about another of those great shines, boy?"

I gave him my best shines, probably the best I had ever given.

He nodded and smiled. He overpaid me and

asked, "Have you been eighty-sixed from any speaks lately?"

I just laughed. Stelfox came over and told Chies what had happened. Both men laughed.

I put away my shine box and reopened Stelfox's betting books.

"Does he always do your books for you?" Aldo asked Stelfox.

"As often as possible. He's damn good and works cheap."

Chies nodded and smiled. "Work hard and stay honest, Francis. You'll do O.K. in your business career." He left, got into his big fine car and took off.

You'll do O.K. in your business career. I grinned, thinking of his compliment. Yeah, big man, I'll do just fine—I'll gamble with other people's money, just like you do. Only I'll have a bigger home and fancier cars.

But then I went back to work and temporarily forgot about my huge dreams. Soon enough the clock said it was time for me to go home.

Vancouver was one of the world's rainiest cities, so it didn't surprise me at all when the sky started pissing down on me. I didn't want to go back to the orphanage for dinner, so I went to Granville Street and dropped into Amnon's father's drugstore. Amnon came right up to me, smiling. "Francis! Glad to see you! Want a root beer float?"

"Yummy," I said as we walked over to the soda fountain. We slurped down cur floats and I could have easily have downed another one but didn't want to seem greedy. We sat there and talked. He said he was a year my junior but in the same grade because he had skipped ahead due to being very smart. I nodded; he seemed like a bright boy. Presently a girl came up to us.

"Amnon," she said, "we'd better get going or we'll be late for dinner."

"Francis," he said, "this is my sister Yael."

We shook hands and said hi. I thought she was a lovely blonde girl with a fine figure and a big dimpled smile.

Amnon told her about that afternoon, and I guess she got the idea that I had picked on him, because she just walked away without saying goodbye.

"Maybe she thought you were bullying me today," he said. "Listen, I got some boxing gloves at home. You want to put 'em on and show me how to fight? You probably know by now that I can't fight for shit."

"When? Tonight?"

"Yeah, tonight. You go home for dinner and afterwards come to my place and we can spar."

"Negative," I said, shaking my head. "I live in the orphanage. If I go there for dinner, they'll lock the doors and I won't be able to get out for the evening."

"Too bad." Then, "Wait a minute. Maybe I can fix things. I think I really need to learn to fight and you're the one to teach me. I don't want anyone calling me names again. Let me talk to my dad." He went off and spoke to his father at the back of the store. He came back and said, "It's a done deal. You'll have dinner with us and then we'll box."

I really didn't want to but nodded yes.

His parents had stepped out for the evening, so it was just Amnon, Yael and me. We ate dinner, which their maid, Anya, had made for us. She was a young woman from back east; she spoke with a weird accent. She ate with us, and we were all hungry, so we ate fast and were soon done. Amnon felt eager to begin our boxing lesson, so we went into his father's den, which was a big, fancy room that looked too nice for boxing lessons.

We laced up our gloves and I said, "Ready to go?"

He nodded. I assumed a fighting stance and said, "Lead with your left. Always protect yourself." Then, "Just try to hit me. Do your best."

"I don't want to hurt you."

"That's your problem. The bullies love bugging you because they know you don't want to hurt them. But *they* want to hurt *you*."

He dropped his left and swung with his right. I blocked it without any effort. "Bad move. You dropped your left and left yourself wide open. I could have knocked you cold just now."

"Oh." For a few minutes he kept his left up and then he didn't. I let him throw a few roundhouse punches that missed badly. Then he stopped fighting.

We looked at each other for a moment and started boxing again. Just then Yael entered the room and Amnon looked away from me. I punched him in the eye and down he went.

"You punched out my brother!" Yael screamed. "You bastard! You're bigger than he is. Why don't you punch out someone your own size?"

"Didn't mean to do it," was all I could say.

Amnon got up and said, "Not his fault. He was just trying to teach me to defend myself."

"Your eye is already getting black and blue," said Yael.

Then Anya entered the room. She said, "You need to get some ice on that eye to keep down the swelling."

"Sorry, Amnon," I said.

"I sort of asked for it," he replied, laughing. He took off his gloves and said, "We'll have another lesson when I'm ready." He left the room. Yael was gone, too.

Anya picked up Amnon's gloves and put them on. "Teach me to box. My father said I should have been a boy. I've always been a tomboy."

"I'm glad you're a girl," I said.

"Don't hit me. I'm afraid of getting punched—especially here." She tapped her breasts. I swallowed hard.

"Well, just take a few good swings at me and then we'll quit."

She nodded and held out her arms quite awkwardly. She threw a few ridiculous punches that I easily blocked. Anya moved in much closer and threw harder punches. Soon I clinched her. She was tall and voluptuous and I felt my cock stiffen.

"You're very strong," she said.

"You're very beautiful."

She smiled. "I can see that you like me."

I felt my face redden. Then we noticed that Yael was in the doorway watching us. We broke our clinch right away.

"I was just showing her how to box," I said.

"That right, eh?" retorted Yael.

"You say that like you don't believe me."

"Time for you to go." She walked me to the door. "Mind doing me a favor?"

"Name it," I said.

"Stay away from Amnon."

"Because…?"

"Because with friends like you, who needs enemies?"

I smirked. "Goodnight, Yael." She shut the door in my face and I sauntered down the hallway. Another door opened and Anya popped her head out. "Hey, you," she said in a hoarse whisper.

"Who, me?"

"Yes, you. Get your ass in here."

I nodded and did as told. We were in her little apartment within the building. She said, "I'm not supposed to have boys in here. We must be very silent."

She needn't have admonished me to be quiet; I was so anxious I could scarcely speak. All I could do was look at her and feel my cock harden again. She turned off the light and came over to me. She put her arms around my neck and kissed me. After a few moments she slipped her tongue into my mouth. With my eyes closed I reached down past her back and groped her lovely young buttocks. We tumbled together onto her bed.

"Oooh, you're so big and strong," she whispered. "Please don't hurt me, please don't." Then, "Oh, please hurt me, please make me suffer…"

At just after midnight I left. Walking down the warm, we streets, I felt like a man. But no, I was not a man, I was a fool, a boy. I was big for my age but still had much growing up to do. I was a big-headed boy with a big smart mouth.

Chapter 6

Tommy Stelfox had given himself the day off and left me in charge of the poolroom. He had driven his wife and kid down to the train station so they could go out to the country for the summer.

I had all the tables ready for use and had put myriad bottles of beer in buckets of ice for consumption later. I had swept the floor clean. As I labored away, Clark and Cal came by.

"Working hard or hardly working?" they asked me.

"Everyone's a comedian. The old man's out for the day. Come on in."

"Kids aren't allowed. It's for adults only," Cal said.

"We won't tell anyone," I said.

"O.K. if we shoot some pool?" Cal asked.

"No, it's against the law for kids to use the pool table. If the cops came in and saw you guys playing pool..."

"Want to go swimming with us?" Clark asked.

"That would be fun. Come by later on when Tommy's here. If business is slow, he'll let me go with you."

That afternoon was hot and Stelfox came in sweating. But he was also smiling. He said, "My wife and kid are in the country now! Yea for me!" He let me take off to go swimming.

The three of us skedaddled. On our way down the street we spotted Amnon. I called out to him. He ran over to us and I introduced him to Clark and Cal and he agreed to go swimming with us.

When we reached the pool, we said, "Damn! Too crowded!" But we stripped naked and dived in anyway. The water was cold and clean but reeked of chlorine and too many people.

Clark said, "If you had said yes to summer in the country with me, we wouldn't have to share our swimming space with a zillion others."

Presently we climbed out of the pool and went outside to lay in the sun. Vancouver was a priceless place on a beautiful day, and today was beyond beautiful. I sprawled out and closed my eyes, fantasizing about my future and all the good times that awaited me in life.

Suddenly someone blocked out my sunshine and stood over me. "Who let this freakin' kike swim in this community pool?"

I thought the guy was speaking of Amnon so I just lay there and played it cool.

"Hey, guys," he said, "come over and take a look at a real live naked Jew!"

His friends came over and cackled. "There should be a law against Jews' being naked in public, eh?"

The first guy said, "Hey, Hymie, we want to see what they rest of you looks like. How about giving us a peek."

I then felt my leg being kicked. The first guy said, "Hey, Jewboy, when I say, 'Jump!' you say, 'How high, sir?' When I say, 'Show us the rest of your ugly Jewish body,' you get up and show us."

I sat up and opened my eyes. Steve, Cal and Amnon were sitting nearby, wondering how we were going to get out of this one. Those bullies could see that I had been circumcised, which was why they thought I was Jewish. Amnon already had his jeans on, so they couldn't see his dick. "My name is Stone," I said. "Francis Stone. I'm not Jewish. Now get out of my face."

"He's telling the truth," one of the bullies said. "He's a bastard from the orphanage."

I stepped towards the guy who had just called me a bastard. He threw up his hands. "I don't have a beef with you. I didn't mean to offend you. It's just that I don't like Jews coming to this pool. If I saw a Jew here, I would kick his ass in two minutes."

Just then Amnon spoke up. "I'm a Jew. Are you going to kick my ass?"

The bully was a bit bigger than Amnon, who had his back to the bad guy. When the bully charged at him, Amnon sidestepped him and the bully charged past him. His own momentum carried him into the swimming pool, which probably displeased him because he was dressed in street clothes.

"The kike fooled you, eh?" I said as I stood at the edge of the pool. The bully yelled some profanities as he pulled himself out of the water. Just then someone yelled, "A woman's coming in," and those of us who were still naked jumped into the pool.

Soon afterwards the woman went away and we got dressed. "I need to get back to work," I said as I headed off in the direction of Tommy Stelfox's pool hall.

Clark walked me back to my destination. He said, "Don't forget that you're going to meet my father after church tomorrow."

I walked in and saw Stelfox, who was hot and sweaty and busy. He shouted at me, "Go downstairs and get some cold beers. We got a bunch of thirsty customers here."

Chapter 7

Stelfox's pool hall was closed every Sunday because a Vancouver bylaw said so. As an altar boy, I had to stay at the orphanage through all the Masses. The last one would end at about noon and I would usually go back to the orphanage, have dinner then go out and goof off for the rest of the day. Sometimes I would go to a movie or do some window shopping downtown and daydream of all the fancy, shiny things I would buy once my ship came in. Today, of course, was different; I had promised Clark I would go with him to see his father.

Steve's father was the mayor of Vancouver—a career politician, devout democrat, regular guy, man of the people. I disliked him. My contempt for him started way back—long before I had made friends with his son. Mr. Rutledge was some hotshot from our district and he came to our orphanage to deliver a speech. Most of us kids understood very little of his speech because we were too full of hot turkey, pumpkin pie and ice-cold milk to pay much attention to him. I was nine at that time. He asked me to go into the office to get some cigars from his overcoat pocket and bring them to him. When I handed over his stogies, he handed me a big bright shiny quarter and said, "Thank you for being such a nice boy."

"Thank you," I said. Then I remembered what the church had taught us—that what was ours was also theirs—and put the quarter into the collection box.

"Well, that's very kind of you, young man. What's your name?"

"Francis Stone, sir."

"Well, Francis Stone, here's a five-dollar bill for you to put into the box. But first, tell me: what do you want for Christmas?"

"An electric train set, sir."

"Well, then, that is what you will get." He beamed as I deposited the fiver into the church box.

I waited with the utmost eagerness for Christmas Day. That morning I ran down the steps towards the huge Christmas tree in the living room, half-expecting to see that train set; alas, my gift was not there. I told myself that maybe the delivery man, or Santa Claus, or whoever was responsible for delivering the train set simply hadn't gotten to us yet. By the end of the day my present was still absent.

My heartbreak hadn't really set in till I went to bed on Christmas night. Then I bawled into my pillow. Brother Lawrence heard me as he walked down the hallway. He came in and asked me what was the matter. I sat up and told him.

He nodded and listened. "Francis," he said, "don't be cryin' about such little things as that. Be grateful for such good things as you have and the good things you have to look forward to in the years ahead. It could be that Mr. Rutledge is a very busy man who just didn't have time to buy you that train set."

He stood and smiled down at me. "Better get some sleep because tomorrow we'll be going sleigh riding in Stanley Park. If you'll look out the window you'll see it's been snowing."

Brother Lawrence left and I got up to look out the window. He told the truth; big fat flakes floated down everywhere. Vancouver had had a white

Christmas that day, and our city was known for *wet* Christmases, not white ones. I smiled at the sight of it and crawled back into bed. I heard Brother Lawrence in the hallway saying in a hushed voice, "I can live with those politicians lyin' to everyone about everything just to get elected, but I hate it when the buggers lie to little boys and break their hearts."

Then the hallway light flickered and died, and I lay in bed hating Chip Rutledge with all the bitterness and heartbreak in a little orphan boy's soul.

When I first met Steve, not long before his father became Vancouver's mayor, I didn't know what to make of him. I liked him despite myself and could see right away that he had no idea that his father had transferred him from some ritzy private school to St. Anthony's because of a weird thing called "public relations."

My way of greeting him was to try kicking his ass. Soon after squaring off, we both realized that our fight would become a draw because he, like me, was a fairly big, tough kid who knew how to fight. I couldn't take him, so I held out my hand and shook his. We became friends right away.

He didn't know why I abruptly ended our fistfight and introduced myself to him—maybe he thought I was a little weird and crazy, and I guess maybe I was—but we became the best of friends and hung out together all the time. He didn't know that I disliked his father, or that Hizzoner and I had ever even met—and I really didn't see that it was any of Steve's business, anyway. I kept wishing Clark would stop inviting me out to the country, but he kept after me about it, and right after the last Mass, there he was.

"Ready?" he asked me.

"Yeah."

"Then let's go," he said.

So we did. Presently we arrived at his front door. A butler opened it for us. "Hello, Master Steve."

"James, where's my father?"

"He's waiting for you in the library."

We went into the library and said hello to Mr. and Mrs. Rutledge. He had his big smile on that rarely left his face. His wife had a gentler, kinder face.

"So, there you are, Steve!" said Chip Rutledge. "It seems you're so busy these days that we need to make an appointment just to say hello."

"Well, here I am," Clark replied, "and here's my pal Francis."

The mayor and his missus turned to have a look at me. Suddenly I felt like the raggedy orphan boy I truly was.

"Pleased to meet you, Francis," said Chip Rutledge, coming over and shaking my hand.

I don't remember what I said then, or if I said anything at all, but then the butler came in and announced that lunch was ready. We all went in to chow down.

After lunch we returned to the library. Mr. Rutledge said, "Clark tells me he wants you to go to the country with him."

"Yessir. But I can't do it."

"Why not?"

"Because I have a summer job."

He frowned. "You have the rest of your life to punch a clock and go to work. At your age, you should spend your summer splashing around in a lake out in the country."

I nodded. "But I need money. I'll be a teenager soon and I'm getting tired of relying on charity. I want to start feeling independent."

Soon they left the room, leaving Clark and me alone. After staring at each other for a few minutes, we went upstairs to his bedroom. Then he said, "Let's go up to the attic. We've gotten it all fixed up."

"Let's do that," I said.

Upstairs I discovered his electric-train set. "Wow!" I said. "Just wow!"

"Nice, eh? Want to play with it for a while?"

I swallowed hard. "I think I would rather go swimming."

Chapter 8

I was going to start high school that September. Clark was going to Elizabeth High on the West Side, so I decided to go there too. Amnon had also decided to attend Elizabeth. I didn't know what to study once high school started. I also supposed it didn't matter much. British Columbia law said that once a student turned fifteen he could withdraw from school without parental consent, so I decided I would tough it out till my fifteenth birthday, then leave Elizabeth and do what I really wanted to do, which was to become a rich gambler and bookie.

Our graduation ceremony at St. Anthony was quick and easy. Friends and family showed up, we sat through a few speeches and were handed diplomas and it was a done deal.

When they called my name, I stepped onto the platform and received my diploma from the Monsignor, who had arrived exclusively for this occasion. Then I returned to my seat and sat with my classmates. Afterwards I sat there and watched as my classmates and their families hugged and kissed and beamed at each other.

I suppose I really felt sorry for myself on that day. I saw Clark and his family. Plenty of people surrounded them, and they blocked his view of me; otherwise he would have waved me over. Soon I began wandering over to the doorway. It looked as if no one in the room had much use for me, and I thought I might be more comfortable outside. Just then someone tapped my shoulder. I looked around and saw Brother Lawrence smiling at me. With him was Father Slovick, and both were beaming at me.

"Congratulations!" they said at once.

I nodded and smiled. I had a lump in my throat. I couldn't speak. When was the last time anyone had said "Congratulations!" to me?

"Didn't think we were goin' to be here, eh?" asked Brother Lawrence.

"Well…"

"It wouldn't do for us to be absent on this special day of one of our boys, would it, Father?"

Father Slovick shook his head. "It wouldn't do at all. We're quite proud of you, Francis."

"Thank you, thank you," I managed to say.

Brother Lawrence put his hand on my shoulder as we walked towards the door. I began to feel like my usual happy self. Outside, Father Slovick shook my hand, wished me luck and headed back towards the church. Brother Lawrence and I returned to the orphanage.

When we reached the courtyard, he turned to me and handed me a gift. His manner seemed somehow uncomfortable, as if he had given few gifts and did not especially enjoy doing so. "This is for you, Francis."

I accepted the package and opened it. Inside sat a gold wristwatch with a leather strap. Right away I put it on and admired it.

"Do you like it?" he asked me.

"It's wonderful." I wiped away a tear.

He smiled at me and I at him. Together we walked into the big gray building.

Chapter 9

That summer was the first time I had socialized on a consistent basis. I learned to get along with people--to joke and laugh, to talk and listen, to hear opinions that were different from mine and not get mad at the person for disagreeing with me. I learned many things that summer, and Anya taught me most of them.

The day after my graduation ceremony, I had dinner with Amnon.

He met me at the door. "My parents are out for the evening, so it'll just be us. Want to do some boxing after dinner? Or we can goof off. Whatever you want."

I nodded. "Boxing or whatever is fine."

We immediately put on the gloves and began sparring. Anya poked her head in the door and said, "Dinner's ready."

"O.K.," I said, pulling off my gloves. To Amnon I said, "You're sweating like a pig. Better take a shower."

"Good idea."

I went into the kitchen. Anya said, "Where is he?"

"Taking a shower." I looked her up and down and reminded myself of what a pretty girl she was.

"How are the boxing lessons coming along?" she asked.

I shrugged. "I guess he's making progress. But he's a fairly big, tough guy. I'm not sure he needs these lessons. I think he needs a pal to hang out with. He doesn't seem to have too many friends."

"Do *you* have many friends?"

"I have a large number of roommates at the orphanage who probably think they're my friends."

"Am *I* your friend?" she asked, wrapping my arms around her waist. I held her close. She was warm and her body felt good. I could feel her breasts pressed against my chest. It flattered me a great deal that she found me attractive. When, in my most private moments, I tried to figure out my strengths and weaknesses, I lately discovered that girls thought I was a handsome boy they wanted to kiss, and that was a special quality I had that many other boys my age didn't have.

"Do you like kissing me?" she asked.

"It's not so bad."

"We should kiss some more."

"If you say so."

"You're younger than I am, Francis," she said, "but in some ways you're already a man. You're bossy and hard and tough. You're rough around the other boys—they're all afraid of you—but with me you're gentle and soft. Tell me that you love me, Francis Stone."

"I really like you a lot."

"Not good enough. Say, 'I love you, Anya!' Say it!"

I almost did, but then Amnon entered the room and I half-pushed Anya away.

"So—what's goin' on?" asked Amnon.

"Nothing," I muttered, wiping the memory of Anya's kiss from my lips.

We sat down to eat. Before long, Yael came in. She said, "Sorry I'm late, Anya, but we ran a little long at the club—we're electing a new board of directors, you see." She glowered at me. "Are you here again?"

"Yeah. You got a problem with that?"

Anya brought Yael her plate and then sat down to eat with us. Anya could doubtless sense the fact that Yael and I did not especially like each other.

After dinner we went into the parlor for a little while. I left at just after eight-thirty. Yael walked me to the door and said, "I see you chose not to follow my advice."

"Oh? Did you offer me some advice?"

"To stay away from Amnon."

"Yeah, I decided o keep being his friend. If you don't like it, you can kiss my ass."

"I hate you! I hate how you're unlike other boys your age. You're so cold and hard and mean. I can't help but think you're spending so much time with my brother because you want to take advantage of him."

I had nothing to say so I said nothing. I just turned and walked away. Anya, on the other side, stood waiting for me.

"Well, finally! I thought you would never get here!"

"The long wait is over," I said, following her into her room. Right away I grabbed and kissed her, then tried to push her down onto the bed.

"Say 'I love you' first." Her voice was without levity; her features were stiff and cold.

"I love you, Anya," I said, pulling her into a tight embrace.

Chapter 10

"Listen up," said Tommy Stelfox. "This will be the easiest gig you've ever had. Your whole territory will be most of downtown Vancouver. My customers are expecting you. All you need to do is take their bets, write them down and bring them to me before the races are run. If you can't get back here on time, call me and give me the information you have. We'll run your book on a split. As long as you're ahead, we'll split the money evenly. When you're in the red you'll have to get back into the black before we split again."

"You're the boss," I said. We'd had this conversation many times; over the past few minutes he had said nothing new. I felt eager to get started. I tapped my pad of paper and racing forms and headed for the door.

Tommy shouted, "Just remember not to accept any markers except for those I approve. And remember to call if you can't get back here on time."

"I hear you, Tommy," I replied as I stepped through the doorway. Outside, the street felt bright and hot. Vancouver in summer was supposed to be like Vancouver in winter—gray and rainy. I wasn't sure how much I liked this hot weather. Tommy had lent me his address book; I looked at it and saw that my stop was a garage in the West End run by some guy named Kelly. I walked out that way and found the garage fast enough.

Inside the place, the air was cool. A big Native guy stood washing cars. "I'm looking for Kelly," I said.

"I'm Kelly," he said. "What do you want?"

"Tom Stelfox sent me."

"You got what I want?" he asked.

"Right here." I handed him the paper. He called out, "Hey, Rick, the bookie's here."

I smiled. Being called "the bookie" made me feel that these guys were taking me seriously. From the darkness another Native man appeared. He eyed me up and down, clearly unused to doing business with someone so young, but when I simply stared at him and straightened up to my full height, he started looking at the sheet with Kelly. They muttered at each other, nodded, shook their heads and tapped the paper. Then Kelly said, "Come here, kid."

I did as told and held my pencil and paper pad, ready to write names and numbers.

"Want to go half and half?" Kelly asked Rick.

"Let's do it," replied Rick.

To me, Kelly said, "O.K., kid, we'll do some business with you. Tomorrow your boss will be broke."

"As long as it's him and not me," I retorted.

Both men laughed.

"Give me fifty cents on Rocket and Macho Fellow for the daily double," Kelly said, "and fifty cents win and place on Bad Girl. I have a good feeling about this, and if I'm right..."

"Gotcha," I said, writing it down. "Anything else?"

He shook his head. "That's enough for today. But if these bets win like I think they will, you'll be coming by tomorrow with a pile of cash, and then we'll really do some heavy betting." He returned the sheet to me.

"Well, if your winnings turn out to be as big as you think, I'll just call you and ask you to come by to pick up your money in a truck," I said.

"That can be arranged," he said, handing me two dollars, which I put into my pocket with much care.

"See you tomorrow," I said as I walked out the door.

My next stop was a delivery entrance on Smithe Street that ha a big loading platform raised three feet above the ground. I saw two trucks backed up against it. Men sat around eating sandwiches and smoking cigarettes. I walked up to one of them.

"I'm looking for Joe Gauthier," I told him.

"Joe's over by the elevator door," he said, pointing at a tall man not far away.

"Thanks," I said. I walked over to him and said, "Are you Joe Gauthier?"

"Who's asking?"

"Tommy Stelfox sent me."

"Let's go over there," he said. "I don't want the boss to know what I'm up to."

We disappeared into the corridor, then into the washroom. He took the sheet from me and locked himself in a stall. "Nothing good here today," he muttered.

"One of 'em has to win," I said.

"Last week, every horse I bet on is still running," he told me.

"Maybe this time out will be better."

"Maybe." He went silent for several moments, then said, "All right, give me a dollar place on Criminal in the second race and two to win on Home Run."

"O.K.; anything else?"

He came out of the stall and handed me back the sheet. Then he dug through his pockets for money, finally found it and gave it to me. I nodded and said goodbye. He did not reply.

My next stop was a drugstore not far from Joe Gauthier's workplace. The people at the drugstore bet three dollars; a bit later, some men at a restaurant placed their bets and handed me seven dollars. From there I went to beauty parlors, candy stores, more shops and garages, all the while stuffing other people's money into my own pockets. My last stop was at a rooming house. I rang the bell and a black girl opened the door.

"Is Miss Jillian in?" I asked.

"Who wants to know?" Then, "Well, yes, she's here...but you look kind of young to be wanting to visit with her."

Presently we went upstairs. The colored girl said, "Is Miss Jillian available?"

"Come in," said a female voice.

I went in. Several women sat around in kimonos and robes. The room reeked of perfume and something I would recognize—much later—as a female odor.

"I'm Jillian," said a tall, dark-haired woman. "You want something?"

I nodded. "Stelfox sent me." I figured out that I was in a brothel.

"Good," she said. "Do you have the sheet?"

I gave one to her and the other to another lady. I stood there and tried my best not to stare at them. Finally one of them invited me to sit, so I plopped down into a chair and looked out the window and gazed at the Vancouver street. I got nineteen dollars in bets there. I looked at my new watch and saw that it was nearly two o'clock. I needed to hurry back to

Stelfox's or I would be late. I ran like hell.

"Well, how did it go?" he asked me.

"It went great," I said, taking out the betting slips and putting them on the counter. We totaled up those slips. They amounted to $51.50 in bets. I gave Stelfox all the money and then started cleaning up the place. The afternoon went by fast. As soon as I finished adding up Stelfox's I did my own. There was $22.50 profit in my book. After Stelfox got his cut, I got $11.25.

Eleven dollars and twenty-five cents for one day's work, I said to myself as I walked back to the orphanage for the night. *That's more than I have ever made in an entire week*. Working for Stelfox sure beat the hell out of going to the country for the summer.

Chapter 11

By the end of my first week in my new job I had earned fifty-one dollars. Plus, he paid me six dollars to clean up his pool hall. My wages totally fifty-seven dollars, which was more than most families made in my neighborhood. I guess that back then I really did not appreciate the value of money. I spent some of mine on junk food and pop. For the very first time in my young life, I always had money in my pocket. The kids in my neighborhood all got to gorge on goodies that I paid for. Yes, I was quite a big shot with the roll of bills in my pocket.

I had a swimming date with Anya after church. When we met up I saw that she had a small bag. "What's in there?" I asked.

"My swimsuit. Where's yours?"

"I'm wearing it."

"What will you do after swimming, when your suit is soaking wet?"

"Gee, I don't know."

She grinned. "Well, we'll just have to put yours in here with mine." We were downtown and, like so many others, took the trolley to English Bay to escape the oppressive and unseasonal heat.

When we reached our destination, we rented lockers at a small bathhouse right by the beach. I had a large amount of cash in my pocket so I bought a cheap plastic waterproof belt with a zippered compartment and put my money in it, then wore the money belt over my swimsuit. I walked over to the beach and waited for her. Presently she emerged in her red one-piece swimsuit and she looked fine, really lovely. She was one of the prettiest girls I had ever met, and I liked the idea that we would spend the day together and everyone would think we were a couple.

The water felt refreshing and we splashed around a bit. Then we lay on the beach under the fierce sun.

"How's your job?" she asked.

"Going great and getting even better. I made fifty-one dollars last week."

She gave out a delighted little cry.

"Want to see it?" I pointed at my white plastic

money belt.

"That's O.K.; I believe you." Then, "What are you going to do with it?"

I shrugged. "Spend most of it on myself. Get some clothes that actually fit. I'm sick of wearing hand-me-downs. I want to pick out something that's brand-new and tells the world who Francis Stone is and what he's about." I took out my package of cigarettes and lit one. I offered her one and she lit up too.

"You," she said, taking a deep drag of her cigarette, "should open a bank account. Put away some of that money and just forget it's even there."

I laughed. "Who the hell cares about bank accounts? I'm not going to college; I'm going to become a bookie and make real money. And you're going to be my girl."

She smirked. "I thought I was already your girl."

I smirked, too. "Yeah. You are. And you're going to keep being my girl." I wanted just then to lean over and kiss her, but there were far too many people around. I could be shy with girls when there were people around.

The day before he went to the country, Clark came by the pool hall to see me. "I sure wish I could talk you into going to the country with me, Francis," he said.

"I can't do it. I have this job here..."

"Yeah, but if you change your mind, send me a card at the country place and my dad will send someone to come get you."

"I'll do that. Enjoy your summer, Steve."

He sighed. "I'll try."

We shook hands and he walked away, all hangdog. I envied him more than he could have possibly guessed. I imagined it must have been nice for him, being the son of the mayor of Vancouver, a kid who could get just about whatever he wanted just by snapping his fingers. I went into the washroom and started cleaning it out. As soon as I finished that I needed to go out and see my customers. I had followed Anya's advice and started a bank account over at the Bank of Toronto on Granville Street. I had just about ended my second week as a runner and my bank balance was seventy dollars. My book had been hit for about eighty dollars yesterday, and I needed to overcome that deficit before I got any more profits. I didn't feel especially worried; an occasional hit was good for the bookies as well as for the players. If the player won and got back a little of his losses, he would just bet that much heavier and would end up losing twice as much.

I walked across town and met up with Amnon and Steve. They said they were going swimming and invited me to join them, but I said I had to work. Amnon asked me to visit him at home that evening and I said I would try but could not guarantee that it would happen. A couple of other kids called to them, so Amnon and Clark went off to join them. I continued on my way to the garage; just before I reached my destination I encountered some boys tossing around a football. One of them threw it wide and I caught it; I threw it back.

When I entered the garage, I shouted, "Kelly, where are you?"

He slid out from under a car, smiling. "Hey, Francis. I guess you have something for me."

"I've got twenty-one dollars for you." I paid him

off. He and Rick looked at the day's sheet and bet six instead of their usual two.

In some ways that day just didn't have its usual satisfaction and fulfillment. Some days I made money, and on other days I lost money, and this was one of those days when I paid it out instead of taking it in. On my way back to the pool hall I stopped by the pool and loitered at the fence, watching as the kids dived, splashed, laughed and hollered. I wanted more than anything to strip naked and jump in with them, but I had business to do with Tommy Stelfox.

Someone standing behind me said, "Looks like they're having fun, eh?"

I turned around. Standing there was Aldo Chies. "More fun than *I'm* having…"

He laughed. "Paid out a few dollars today, eh?"

I nodded.

"Right now you would just love to go swimming with them and have no cares in this world. Well, a kid your age should be carefree. Unfortunately, you have a job, a boss to answer to and very little time for swimming with other kids. You're becoming a man very quickly—and being a man often means giving up childish pleasures. Do you know what I see when I look at you? I see myself when I was your age. I was growing up fast and had to learn to work first and play later—and not play at all if there wasn't enough time to play."

I nodded. "You're right, Mr. Chies. I don't feel like those kids anymore."

"That's because you're not a kid anymore. Where are you going?"

"Back to the pool hall."

"I have my car. Let me drive you there. Then you can give me one of your great shoeshines."

We got into his car. I felt pretty good about things as we cruised through the Vancouver streets on our way to Stelfox's. I had great fun walking in there with the big man by my side; I liked it that Tommy knew Aldo and I were friends. Tommy respected Aldo and feared him quite a bit.

Once we reached Stelfox's, I gave Tommy the slips and cash. Then I got out my shine box and said to Aldo, "Ready?"

Aldo nodded and I got to work. "Good kid," he said to Tommy.

Stelfox nodded. "He'll go far. Great work ethic."

When I was done, Aldo handed me a dollar bill.

"It's only fifty cents," I told him.

"Inflation. Your price just went up."

I shrugged and put away the money.

"Francis," Tommy said, "go get Mr. Chies and me a cold beer." To Aldo he said, "I owe you money." Tommy took out a fat roll of bills and counted six hundred dollars. Aldo stuck it into his pocket without counting it.

I left them to go get the mop and pail and wash the tile floor in front of the counter. The unexpected June heat was so oppressive that I took off my shirt and wiped the sweat off my face. When Chies left he waved at me and I waved back. I felt like saying to him, "If you're so powerful, why can't you make this heatwave go away?"

Chapter 12

No, even Aldo Chies couldn't stop our Vancouver heatwave. It was quite unlike any weather we could remember: Hot, muggy, relentless. People traipsed home from work, listless and lethargic. Everyone kept hoping for the rain to come back.

Myself, I liked that summer, except for the heat. I loved how, for the first time in my life, I was my own man, earning my own living and not being some orphan and charity case everyone pitied. By late August I had seven hundred dollars in the bank. I had a girlfriend and two new suits. I ate in restaurants and always had plenty of walking-around money stuffed into my pockets. I could go where I wanted and do the things that gave me pleasure. People I knew, and especially the kids, admired and respected me as a *somebody*. I was living well. As September grew nearer, I began to think about having to go back to school. I didn't want to go; I wanted to keep making big money as a bookie; but I knew I had to continue my academic education. I wasn't old enough to withdraw. My biggest mental challenge was thinking of ways to continue making book while reading textbooks. I felt full of pity for the kids in the orphanage and throughout the neighborhood. Too bad for them that they weren't lucky enough to be me!

I will never forget August 22' of that year. I had just squared up with Stelfox and had eighty-four dollars in my pocket. The pool hall was full of men carrying on—swearing, shouting, farting and smoking. Soon they would all be sauntering out the door to get ready for dates with their wives and girlfriends. We had already sold out of beer and pop. Stelfox turned to me and said, "I'm beat to shit. I think I'll close up and go see the wife."

"Want me to give these guys the bums' rush?"

"Yeah, you do that."

I walked around the tables and called out, "Closing time."

Everyone grumbled and shuffled out the door. Stelfox counted all the cash and stuck it into his pocket. "Let's leave."

As Stelfox stood locking the door, Aldo Chies' car cruised up to the curb. Aldo got out and walked up to Stelfox. "Closing early, Tommy?"

"Yeah. I'm lonely. Gonna go see the wife for the weekend."

"Nice for you. Got anything for me?"

"Always." He squeezed the wad of bills, which he had secured with a big, thick elastic. They stood in the doorway of the pool hall and I stepped away, to give them their space.

I heard the low hum of a motor in the street behind me. Aldo and Stelfox looked up and seemed to be staring in wide-eyed horror at something behind me. I felt no peculiar sensations of any kind but Stelfox went white as chalk and dropped his wad of money.

I reached down and snatched up his money, saying, "You need to be more careful..." Then I heard gunshots and watched as Stelfox grabbed his stomach and dropped to his knees. I watched as Chies clutched at his chest and blood appeared on his clothing. I beat it; I just ran like hell, up one block and down the next. Presently I ended up at Amnon's apartment block. Moments later I pounded on Anya's door, terrified.

When she opened the door I pushed her inside, stepped inside as well and shut it behind us. She saw the blood on my clothing and asked, "Francis, are you hurt?"

I ignored her question; instead, I threw myself onto her bed and groaned.

"Francis! Are you hurt? Tell me or I'll call an ambulance!"

"I'm all right," I said. "The blood isn't mine."

"Then whose is it?"

"They shot Stelfox and Chies tonight."

"Who did it? Why?"

"Some very bad men did it." Just then I noticed that I had Stelfox's wad of cash in my hand. I put it into my pocket, then got up, went over to the window and looked out at Vancouver. "I wonder if those gunmen followed me here," I muttered.

"Francis, your poor guy! You must be scared to death," Anya said, shaking her head.

"Those people don't scare me," I lied. I grabbed her and buried my face in her breasts. She was so soft and warm there; I didn't want to stop. Soon I started shivering and could not stop. My shirt became drenched with perspiration. For the longest time I pressed my face into her beautiful breasts as I shivered and sweated.

By and by I recovered and sat in her overstuffed chair. I said, mostly to myself, "I'm sure no one saw me come here. They were after Chies. They weren't after me. They shot Stelfox because he saw them shoot Chies. I didn't see them shoot Chies so they didn't care about me. Maybe the cops will want to question me. I don't know. What I do know is that if I keep my big yap shut about what I've just seen I will be O.K. Not sure what I'll do with this money, though." I counted it. "Nearly seven hundred dollars."

Anya entered the room with a cup of coffee. "Here, drink this."

I did as told and smiled at her. "I can't leave here with this bloody shirt on. Blood won't wash out, so I'll need to borrow one of Amnon's."

I removed the badly stained shirt and she took it from me. "I'll burn this right away," she said as she disappeared. She came back with one of Amnon's shirts. "Try this on. It's probably a little small."

I put it on. She was right; the shirt was a bit tight. "It'll do," I told her. "I'd better get out of here before the family comes back."

"They're away for the weekend," she said.

I had dinner there and left at about nine o'clock. I headed back to the orphanage and sneaked in, tiptoed into the dormitory, stripped and crawled into bed. I felt comfortable because of that large, delicious dinner I had eaten with Anya, and I could scarcely keep my eyes open once my head hit the pillow. I sank into a long, deep, restorative sleep.

In the morning, I got up before everyone else and went downstairs to check the newspapers. The Vancouver *Times* had given the shooting generous front-page coverage. A two-inch headline fairly yelled, "Chies Shot!" and the story was on page two. I turned the page and found a picture of Chies in the right-hand corner. The story said:

GANG WAR BREAKS OUT IN VANCOUVER

Aldo Chies, infamous gambler and racketeer, was

shot and seriously wounded, and Thomas (Tommy) Stelfox was fatally shot, today by an unknown assailant. Stelfox was shot twice through the heart and Chies was shot once in the chest and in the groin. The incident happened outside a pool hall owned and managed by Stelfox. Police say they are looking for a boy, known to be employed by Stelfox at his pool hall, who may have witnessed the shootings. Chies's condition at a local hospital, according to officials, is serious but not critical. Chies, in the way of comment, said only, "I don't know why anyone would want to shoot me; I'm just a businessman." Police are investigating the case and expect to make progress soon.

I put down the newspaper and decided that Chies's brief comment was an admonition for me to keep my mouth shut just like him. I went into the dining room to have breakfast and then went to church to serve altar. I told myself that all was copacetic; I had nothing to worry about.

Chapter 13

After a week had gone by and nobody had hassled me, I decided that I was perfectly safe. I could walk the streets without fear, and according to the newspapers Chies was recovering rapidly and would be discharged soon from Royal Vancouver Hospital. Stelfox's was padlocked and I was unemployed, but somehow that just didn't seem to matter so much any longer. I had deposited Tommy's fat wad of cash into a separate account and pretty much forgot about it. Anya and I saw each other often and made a point of not discussing that awful evening.

One morning Brother Lawrence poked his head into our dormitory and said, "Francis, will you come to my office after breakfast? We need to discuss something."

I did as told, and when I reached his office Brother Lawrence was there, of course, and so were Sister Superior and Father Slovick, plus a guy who looked like a cop.

I felt worried but tried to play it cool.

"Francis," Brother said, "this is Investigator Franz of child protective services. Mr. Franz, this is the boy we were telling you about."

For a few moments nobody said anything. They made me nervous.

Finally the Sister Superior told me, 'You've been a very good boy in school. I've known you since you were nothing more than a baby. Now I have something to say to you which I don't want to say but feel I must say. Francis, have you ever wanted to be anything except a good Catholic boy?"

"No, ma'am, never," I said.

Father Slovick smiled and said, "That's just what I knew he would say."

"Francis," the Sister Superior continued, "if you were to learn that you were another faith, how would you feel?"

I sighed with relief. This clearly was not about the shooting of Chies and Stelfox. "I'm a Catholic, ma'am. That's all I've ever been."

The adults smiled at each other, as if saying, "See?

110

He's one of us."

"Francis," she asked, "don't you remember anything at all about your parents?"

I frowned. What a stupid question! She knew perfectly well that the orphanage and Catholicism were all I had ever known. "I don't know what you want me to say, ma'am."

"Francis," she said, "Mr. Franz investigates the parents of the children here. His job is to learn as much as he can about the children in order to help them. He has something to tell you."

Mr. Franz shifted his weight from one foot to the other. "You need to understand, Francis, that it all started not long ago, when you graduated from St. Anthony's. Your case came up for review again." He looked down for a few moments and stared at his shoes. "When a child enters secondary school, we again go over his history to see what we can do for him. One of our goals is to locate that boy's family members because our belief is that they're better off with family than with us. Well, it seems we have located a family member of yours—he is your uncle; that is, your mother's brother. Long ago he wrote to

111

us to tell us of his sister who moved to Vancouver on the day you were born. She died just after your birth. He identified her by a ring she owned and we have kept for you. It is not an especially valuable ring but it has sentimental value. Your uncle says you are his nephew and we believe him. He wants you to go live with him. We think he is a good and kind man. He has two children of his own and will do his best to provide you with the best possible home." Mr. Franz went silent.

Father Slovick said, "Francis, you need to understand something. Your uncle is not like us. He is different. He does not believe as we do. He is not of our faith."

I frowned at him. "Not like us? Not of our faith?" I wondered what that actually meant, and wondered if I really wanted to know.

Father Slovick nodded. "Francis, he's not...*Catholic*."

"I thought everyone was Catholic," I retorted.

"Francis," Brother Lawrence said, "it's very much a certainty that you will go live with your uncle soon. We just have to work out some details. Please remember all the good things you have learned here over the years. Remember that Jesus loves you—He always has and always will. Always be a good Catholic and treat others as you would have others treat you."

"Always," I said.

"Your uncle is right outside," said Sister Superior. "Would you like to meet him?"

"Oh, yes, ma'am!" My mind whirred. I found it hard to believe that there were people out there who were mine. I had my own family; I wasn't just some orphan bastard who had to eat, sleep and shit with the other orphan bastards.

Mr. Franz went to the door. "Please come in, Mr. Stein."

A man stepped into the office. He was tall, just over six feet, with broad shoulders and not much hair on his head. He had soft brown eyes and a prominent nose. As I looked him over, I remembered hearing that most Catholics believed that non-Catholics went to hell. Myself, I believed that the world I lived in was hell and that the afterlife, if such a thing existed, was a huge improvement over this life. In all, I decided that a person's religion meant relatively little. We were born, we lived for a while and then we died.

I decided that Mr. Stein seemed like a nice man. He smiled at me; I smiled back.

He shook my hand. "So you're Francis." His voice was deep and resonant, full of warmth and kindness.

"Yessir!" I swallowed hard. I wiped away a tear. I knew now that I had family in this world, that I was not totally alone.

Then it occurred to me that his name was Stein.

Soon I would learn that I was a Jew.

Chapter 14

News sure travels fast. Within a few hours, everyone in the orphanage knew I had been adopted. All the other kids pelted me with questions, but I really didn't have many answers. I eagerly awaited the afternoon so that I could call Anya and tell her the great news.

First I called her to make sure it would be safe for me to go up for a visit. Then I hurried over.

She opened the door to let me in. I noticed she seemed exhausted and lethargic but I didn't especially care about her because all I had on my mind was my adoption news.

She sat on the edge of her bed as I spoke. As soon as I finished, she offered me a weak little smile and said, "I'm glad things are improving for you. Maybe this is the start of a run of good luck."

I furrowed my brow. "I thought you would be much happier."

She sighed. "I'm going home."

"Why? You don't have to leave. I'll still be around to see you regardless of what goes down."

She twisted her mouth. "Why? Because I'm a convenient fuck?"

"No. I see you because I like you. You know I like you because you make me say it all the time."

"You like me," she told me with her chin thrust out, "because I let you feel me up and stick your thing into me. We're over. We'll never see each other again."

"At least explain to me why," I said.

"Because there's nothing in our relationship for me. It's like I'm your main squeeze but not much else. You're so young and full of yourself; you keep forgetting that I'm here. Well, to hell with that. What's in it for me except spreading my legs whenever you get horny?"

I grabbed her arms. "Anya, please don't be like that—"

"Let go of me! Get out!"

I walked over to the door and opened it. "Goodbye, Anya."

She said nothing. I walked away.

Outside, I took out a cigarette and lit it. I listened closely and could swear I could hear her crying on her bed. Women, I thought, shaking my head. Just try to figure them out.

I walked down the street. The sky was clear except for a few scudding clouds and a soft breeze kissed my cheek. On a beautiful day like this Vancouver, everyone agreed, was one of the world's most beautiful cities. Alas, I didn't enjoy this beautiful weather; I felt cold and almost shivered. I wandered into Stanley Park and threw myself onto the grass. I stared up into the sky, past the few clouds, looking up into the endless blue. Anya, I said to myself, Anya, Anya, Anya.

I wrote to Clark and told him I had been adopted. He wrote back that if I was happy, he was happy for me. The weeks went by very fast and soon the day arrived for my departure. That afternoon my uncle would drive to the orphanage to take me to my new home. I had packed my personal possessions into a couple of boxes and stored them for the time being in the superintendent's office.

I didn't want to go back to my room. I listened for a few moments and heard activity in the gym, so I decided to go down to find out what was happening.

Just then I heard the lunch bell ring, so I headed for the dining room, where I bowed my head while Brother Lawrence said grace. At that moment I had the weirdest feeling—that I had never been here till this moment, and that these people and this room were completely unknown to me. I reminded myself that I would soon have a new home. I wondered if my new aunt and cousins would like me. Then I thought maybe I should simply remain at the orphanage.

Brother Lawrence gave me permission to leave the dining room, so I stepped outside. I went into the yard and stood there for several long moments, thinking of the kids I had known, the games we had played, the conversations we'd had. I felt a presence behind me and turned around to see Brother Lawrence.

"You seem a bit out of sorts, Francis," he said.

"I feel strange."

He nodded. "It's to be expected. I've watched you grow for many years, since you were a baby. I saw you when you took your very first steps. When you fell, you had a grim little cast to your mouth as you got up and took another step. But you never gave up, and your determination is still intact. I tried to help you understand people—how to work and play with them, how to get along with them and make friends with them. I tried to be a father and mother to you, but of course that was impossible. I knew you better than you knew yourself. Naturally, there were things I could not tell you—things you needed to learn for yourself. You're doing that right now—growing up and learning for yourself."

I smiled. "Brother Lawrence, you've been wonderful to me. I can't thank you enough."

He smiled enough. "Do not thank me—thank the Church. But I will always feel that I have not taught you enough. Here we teach many good things, but out there—in the real world—is where you will spend the rest of your life. Here at the orphanage we are very sheltered and we protect our boys from the cruel world out there. Nevertheless, it is inevitable that you will inhabit that cruel world and learn to cope with its cruelty." He shrugged. "Anyway, enough with sentiment. Have you said goodbye to Father Slovick, the Sister Superior and all your teachers. They will miss you."

"I've already done that. I'll miss them too." Then, "I have just one more thing to ask you: Is it bad to be a Jew? Does it make me awful?"

Brother Lawrence scratched his head. "Why would you ask such a question?"

"At school, and all around me, people have made fun of Jews. So have I. Now it turns out that *I* am a Jew, too. Does that mean I will burn in hell?"

Brother Lawrence smiled at me. "Francis, as much as we Catholics would like to think the Kingdom of Heaven is ours alone, it is not. People of all faiths are children of God and therefore welcome in His house." Then, "Many Christians quite conveniently forget that Jesus of Nazareth Himself was a Jew."

"Thank you, Brother," I said. "I feel better now."

"Good, because lunchtime is nearly over and I'm famished." He mussed my hair and went inside.

The kids came spilling in from lunch. Soon they surrounded me. I bulled past them and headed into the building through the gymnasium entrance.

I stood there for a few minutes, watching some kids at play. One of them, Peter Costa, stood there shooting baskets. I decided to go over and say goodbye to him and urge him to forget the ridiculous disputes we'd had.

Those kids standing with Peter went quiet as they saw me approach. I could sense that something was wrong but could not say how or why. My heart pounded and pulse raced. Still, I had learned years earlier to play it cool, to hide my emotions. I stopped right in front of Pete and offered him my hand.

"I'm leaving now, Pete. No hard feelings, eh?"

He looked at me and stepped towards me. "No hard feelings my ass." He threw a punch and hit me in the chin. I went down and his friends surrounded me. Pete stood directly over me.

"You goddamn Jew son of a bitch! Coming here every day with us good, clean Christians and not telling anyone!"

Just then Brother Lawrence came rushing up. I

saw Peter's face turn white; he surely thought he had me all to himself for the next while.

"Peter! Why are you mistreating Francis! Explain yourself at once!" Brother Lawrence shouted.

One of the kids blurted out, "Peter said he wanted to teach this dirty kike a bloody lesson!"

"Go away immediately!" Brother Lawrence shouted. To me he said, "Your uncle is here."

Inside the superintendent's office my uncle and aunt sat looking up at me. I did my best to smile.

"I'm Francis Stone...I think."

Interlude

Amnon

Amnon stood at the door, taking a deep breath and enjoying the tinkle of the win chimes. He took off his cap and ran a hand through his thinning blond hair. He looked down at his uniform and decided he had done all right for himself so far. He wondered for a moment what they would be like, and what they would think of him. Four years, it seemed to him, was a long time.

People change in four years. They can change a great deal, he concluded. He himself had been in the business of helping people to change even faster. For four years he had watched boys turn into men—old men, embittered men, men who weren't yet ready for manhood. He had watched them go into war as clueless boys and come out as hardened warriors—or as terrified children who went crazy or killed themselves. Those soldiers could cope with war or they couldn't. Simple as that.

Tina opened the door. Several moments passed as they stood looking at each other. *She hasn't changed much*, he thought. *I suppose that's a good thing.*

"Amnon!" she said with a big, wide smile.

She leaned forward and he closed his eyes, enjoying the soft, smooth warmth of her lips on his own. He wasn't a kisser, hugger or toucher himself, but he enjoyed this moment of innocent intimacy with her.

"Been a little while," she said.

He nodded. "Four years. I was just thinking—"

"How much we had all changed."

"And how much we were going to continue to change."

As she pulled him gently into her living room, he said, "I felt like quite a stranger out there, standing at your front door. In fact, sometimes I feel like a stranger here in Vancouver, the city I was born and raised in."

She nodded as she took his cap and handed it to the maid, who disappeared. Clark hustled into the room.

The two men pumped each other's hand and beamed, two old friends too moved to speak.

"Amnon, you medical man!"

"Steve, you legal eagle!"

Tina disappeared and came back with three glasses of white wine.

"A toast," she said. "To friendship—the kind that lasts more than fifteen minutes."

They laughed and drank.

Over dinner they spoke of Francis, naturally. Tina began reminiscing and Amnon took over.

"The first day I saw him, some kids were picking on me, and he defended me. Damn, he was a tough kid. He feared nobody. I was never able to understand why he liked me or wanted to be friends with me, but I respected him and was glad to have him in my corner.

"In Germany in Nineteen Thirty-five I started to think of him again. I had been studying at one of the big universities, taking specialized courses. One day, coming home from one of the lectures, I was reading a fascinating book as I walked down the street. Reading while walking down the street—smart, eh? Also, that book was written in German, a language with which I was having some difficulty. I bumped into a man, apologized, then went on reading and walking.

"Then I heard him say 'Jude' in a very nasty way. I looked at him and his uniform was unfamiliar to me. He threw a punch at me, and I beat him senseless. Years ago Francis had taught me self-defense, and I remembered most of those lessons. He'd said, 'Pay close attention and learn to fight. I have a feeling you will need to use these skills again and again over the years.'

"I left Germany the day after beating up that guy. I had things to tell people here in Canada about my experiences here and abroad as a Jew; trouble was, only you and a few people others listened and understood. The others said, 'We don't want to hear about it.'"

He laughed and took a sip of wine. "There you have it—the world according to Amnon Lichtmann, the eminent psychiatrist." He smiled, grateful to have friends who listened as he spoke, who did their best to understand him, just as he did his best to understand them.

PART TWO

Chapter 1

I soon learned a great deal about my new family. My uncle worked as a manager of a department store downtown and they had been living in Vancouver for a dozen years. They lived in a comfortable apartment near the University of British Columbia.

His wife, a gentle, soft-spoken woman, was someone I adored immediately. At all times she treated me as a very special young man.

They had two daughters, eight and ten years old. Their girls at first did not know what to make of me and were shy around me. Later, as they got used to having me around, they would kiss my cheek as they came and went.

Daniel and Mabel Stein and their two children, Esther and Pauline, were my first real family, and if we felt strange being together, those weird feelings were understandable. We gave each other space and cut each other slack and, most of the time, functioned as a perfectly viable family unit.

Upon my arrival in their home, I learned that they were going to throw a welcome-to-the-family party for me. Aunt Mabel baked a cake and had many family members over so I could meet them.

Uncle Daniel said, "Francis, this is your bedroom."

Aunt Mabel said, "This is a picture of your mum."

I looked at the woman in the picture. She was scarcely out of her teens, with light hair in a bun, a half-smile, something mischievous but controlled dancing in her eyes. She had full lips, a thin nose, a strong chin. I couldn't decide if I thought she was pretty or plain.

"Here are some pajamas," said Aunt Mabel.

"Thank you, ma'am," I said.

"Call me Aunt Mabel."

"O.K.—Aunt Mabel."

I slept that night with the moonlight on my mother's picture. It seemed to me that she was smiling at me.

Chapter 2

I woke up early the next morning, Everyone else was still asleep. I got out of bed and checked my watch: six-thirty. I stared out the window for the longest time at gray Vancouver.

I took a shower and got dressed. In the hallway I encountered my aunt.

"Good morning, Aunt Mabel," I said.

"You're up early, Francis," she replied.

"An old habit from the orphanage." I missed the horseplay and joking around that usually happened at this hour.

"Well, seeing as how you're dressed, would you mind walking over to the bakery for some rolls? That way I won't have to do it myself."

"Happy to do it."

After I returned, one of my cousins said, "Francis, it's your first day of school. Where are you going?"

"To Oliver Johnson Secondary," I told her.

"That's the biggest high school in Canada," she told me.

Aunt Mabel handed me three dollars.

"I don't need this much," I told her.

"Yes, you do."

Oliver Johnson was a high school on the other side of Vancouver; nevertheless, I found it without much trouble. In my first class, the kid sitting next to me was Indian.

Things were sure different here.

Chapter 3

One can never bring back old times; that was a lesson I learned soon enough. Clark and Amnon and I hung out together sometimes but we just could not recapture the closeness we'd had when I lived at the orphanage. I still valued our time together and considered them my greatest friends, but I had changed in significant ways. I was no longer the outsider looking in; I now had a home and family and my own situation now became the most important thing in my life. At home I cared more about my family than I did myself; outside of home, though, I was still selfish Francis.

Time went by fast. I was a decent student, no better or worse than a hundred others and no desire to distinguish myself among my peers. Still and all, eventually I began to assume a sort of leadership role when dealing with the other boys. Such a development scarcely surprised me; I had expected to do as much. I was bigger than most and much more assertive. I had already forgotten more about sex than these boys had ever learned, and I listened with supreme amusement as they discussed the best ways of seducing a female. A capable athlete, I joined the basketball and swimming teams. In sports, an in life in all its spheres, I played to win. Rules were for dumbasses who didn't know enough to get away with breaking them. I, Francis Stone, truly hated to lose.

At a dance one evening, Amnon approached me with a girl we knew, a nice chick whose name had escaped me.

"Francis," he said, "you're going to be the next class president. You're someone the other kids will vote for—even if they don't always *like* you, they admire and respect you. This girl will be your running mate. As student-body president, you'll mainly just walk around and look very, very important."

Then he walked away. The new girl—my running mate—said, "Francis, do you want to dance?" She had a pretty blonde smile—lots of even white teeth and big dimples.

"Do I want to dance? I guess so…but I don't

know how."

We danced, I stepped on her toes a bunch of times and then we got some punch at the refreshment table.

Soon she said, "It's eleven. Getting late. I have to go home."

I nodded. "I've had a fun time. I didn't think I would."

I kissed her goodnight. She kissed back. She went away, and just then I remembered her name: Tina Lundquist.

Chapter 4

On Christmas week, Clark and Amnon came to my house for a visit. My uncle, aunt and cousins ha gone out for the evening. Mostly we hung out in the parlor.

Naturally, Clark did nearly all of the talking. He wanted me to agree to run for student-body president. Of course, I enjoyed hearing what he had to say. He knew how to appeal to my considerable ego. "It will be a good thing for you. You'll get to sit in on student-teacher committee meetings and get extra credit in civics class."

"Bloody right!" said Amnon. "Besides, you'll be a Big Man on Campus. You're a leader and everyone will listen to you."

"That right, eh? Like, what would I have to do?"

"Just be yourself. You'll have to make a brief speech at the introductory rally on the Friday after we get back to school."

I scowled. "Me? A speech? No. Not gonna

happen."

Amnon laughed. "It's easy. We've already written your speech. You'll just read what we've written. Here's a copy."

He handed it to me. I read it. "This doesn't make sense."

"Doesn't matter," Clark said. "Politics is bullshit. My father has always told me that people get elected because they have charisma, personality, presence. You can have great ideas and good intentions, but you get elected because of your personal qualities."

"Amen to that," said Amnon.

"Well," I said, "if I come off looking like a freakin' fool, the two of you will be to blame."

"Won't happen," Clark said. "We know what we're doing."

For a dozen consecutive evenings I practiced that speech. Amnon and Clark coached me on it till I nearly punched them out.

On the big day, as I sat on stage with all the other candidates, I convinced myself that all the people in the audience were staring at me. Tina Lundquist sat next to me. She smiled at me and tried to smile back, but I was sure I appeared to be wincing.

The principal made his speech, something about this student-body election being a grand opportunity for us students to practice democracy. But I missed most of what I heard because I felt so overcome with anxiety.

The first candidate got up to speak. He promised to give his fellow students the best representation they had ever had, and he took just over ten minutes to have his say. As soon as he finished, he sat down and the cheerleaders got up to give him some rah-rah-rah! Then they quieted down and the second candidate got up. He said pretty much what the first guy had said, in much the same way and he took about the same amount of time. As soon as he got done, the cheerleaders gave him a wiggle, giggle and jiggle. In the audience, the students were fidgeting, spacing and out starting hushed conversations with each other. Presently my turn came, I got up to speak.

My heart pounded; my throat felt parched as I stepped up to the microphone. "Mr. Principal, teachers and fellow students…" My voice seemed to boom halfway across Canada. *Too loud* I thought.

The kids in the audience shook their heads and made faces at me, as if I had just shaken them awake.

"I'm really nervous," I said in a small voice. They all laughed—even the teachers.

"I don't know why I'm up here anyway."

The whole room roared. I could feel my tension evaporating like water from my skin.

"A few days ago, a couple of people—friends of mine—said to me that I should run for student-body president. Like a good, I said, 'O.K.' Now I'm starting to wonder if those people really *were* my friends."

Big laugh. I thought, *Clark was right! They're eating it up!*

"I have listened to my opponents' speeches and am starting to think that maybe I will vote for them."

A big *hahahaha!* filled the room.

"I'm not sure what to promise to do for you. My opponents have already promised things that even the prime minister of Canada couldn't deliver."

They screamed and applauded. I held up my hands to shush them.

"Not that I think they're wrong—on the contrary, I think they're absolutely right. I would love to promise you all the goodies you crave—shorter hours, less coursework and a six-month summer vacation—but I have a feeling the Vancouver School Board might have something to say about that."

More laughs, big laughs. Clark and Amnon sat in the first row; I made the briefest eye contact with them and they gave me discreet thumbs-up.

In closing, I said, "I don't want to say too much more because I know how eager you are to get back to class." Everybody laughed. "But I know one thing: Who ever ends up being elected will do their best to give you the best representation possible. Thank you."

I went back to my seat and sat down. The students jumped out of theirs and applauded.

Tina leaned over to me and mouthed, *Take a bow.*

I nodded, then took her hand and stood. We walked together to the center of the platform and waved. She looked irresistibly pretty in her pink dress.

"If you don't vote for me," I said into the microphone, "at least vote for Tina Lundquist for vice-president. She'll be the prettiest and smartest veep Oliver Johnson has ever had."

The audience applauded and laughed till the bell sounded and rally ended. We walked down the steps from the platform and were greeted by friends and admirers.

That afternoon, as they counted the ballots, Tina and I sat and waited with some friends in the office of the campus newspaper. Yael Lichtmann came up to me while I was saying something to Tina.

"Gee, Francis, that was really great," she said, her voice laden with sarcasm. "Maybe you should audition for the drama club. Mrs. Tunnicliffe would be so impressed." Then she walked away.

"Friend of yours?" Tina asked me.

I shrugged. "She's Amnon's sister."

Just then Amnon came bounding in, breathless with elation. "Guess what? You've both been elected!"

He pumped both our hands for several seconds. I didn't smile—I was still stewing over Yael's smartass remark—but then I laughed.

Presently came hurrying in with a dozen other kids. They made such a fuss over me that I soon forgot about Yael and her nasty remark.

Chapter 5

My peers elected me student-body president, and that was how I came to know Mrs. Tunnicliffe and why Amnon went on to become the man he did. But I am getting ahead of myself.

I became acquainted with Mrs. Tunnicliffe at the first meeting of student council. Mrs. Tunnicliffe, a kindly woman of about fifty with gray hair and blue eyes, was doing some psychological work in connection with the child-welfare department.

At that meeting, most of the problems they spoke of were the usual things: children chronically late or truant, skipping out, talking back to instructors. We did not try to punish them; instead, we tried to figure out who was right or wrong in such conflicts—the student, teacher or student's parents. Every case ended up in Mrs. Tunnicliffe's hands. She would interview the acting-out student and find out the reasons for his misbehavior.

In a school as big as ours, petty infractions happened all the time. Mrs. Tunnicliffe's student assistant, a girl who helped the teacher with her records, graduated that term. So when Mrs. Tunnicliffe asked for another student helper, I suggested that Amnon volunteer his services. I knew he wanted extra credit.

Amnon and she liked each other straightaway, and he liked the work. That experience probably inspired him to pursue psychiatry as a profession. He had long aspired to become a doctor, and people with mental and emotional disorders fascinated him.

Tina and I became very friendly, and around Oliver Johnson Secondary, everyone considered us a couple. I liked her just fine but felt that Anya had been more my type. Still, Tina and I went out on dates, hugged and kissed each other goodnight and attended school functions together. We traipsed through the boring, frustrating process of growing up.

School dragged on. By and by Easter arrived, then summer vacation. I passed all my courses and went to the country with my relatives.

I enjoyed every moment of that summer. Many other young people went to the country and I made some friends. I swam every day and hung out on the beach all day. The sun tanned my skin and bleached my hair blond. I imagine I was very much like the other kids out that way that summer. We ogled the girls in their swimsuits, whispered about their titties and asses and speculated on which did or did not do this or that on the first date.

I gained a few pounds that summer and soon it came time to go back to Vancouver and Oliver Johnson Secondary School. Still, that was easily the finest summer of my life. I sometimes wonder why a few of the details escape me, but so much of it was so much fun that I lost track of time and, far too soon, my trip was over.

Back to school. This year I was in Grade 9, which meant I no longer had to suffer the indignity of being a Grade 8. I made the cut when I tried out for the swimming and basketball teams and began wearing the golden *J* on my sweater. I, Francis Stone, had become a Big Man on Campus, admired and adored by all.

All of us had grown that summer—Amnon, Steve, Tina and yours truly—but I really hadn't appreciated how much till one evening after a football game. I drove her home; she was having dinner with her grandparents and would join them after changing her clothes. I wanted to walk her over there before heading home myself. As she changed I sat in the front room reading the Vancouver *Times*.

Presently she came into the room wearing her bathrobe and carrying a slip over her arm. "It's not dry yet," she said. "I have to iron it. It won't take long."

"I'm in no hurry."

She went over to the window and looked out. "Wow! It's snowing in October!"

I laughed. "Usually it just rains here every other day throughout the year."

"I think I would rather have rain than snow," she said. "At least with rain you don't slip, lose your footing and break your neck on the sidewalk."

I went over to her and slipped my arms around her waist. I kissed her neck.

She turned around and snaked her arms around me. Then she let them drop. "The iron must be hot by now."

"So am I—hot and hard."

She made a face.

I pulled her in close and kissed her again. I could tell she had on very little underneath her bathrobe. I led her to the sofa and we sat down. I kissed her some more.

"Francis, stop," she said, her voice scarcely more than a purr.

"Darling," I murmured. Her hands held my head close to her.

"Francis, Francis, Francis..." Presently she pushed me away and said, "We shouldn't carry on like that. It's beneath us."

"O.K."

She got up and smiled. She got dressed and I walked her to her grandmother's house. She, I said to myself, has grown up, too.

Chapter 6

Just before Christmas I heard about Mac Yale. Although I was on the student-faculty advisory committee I had been absent from all of the hearings he had been called to. That was because I had commitments elsewhere and, anyway, I was a lazy bastard who found those committee meetings boring as hell.

Amnon stopped me in the corridor and asked me to see Mrs. Tunnicliffe that afternoon.

"Why?" I asked him.

"Because it's about Mac Yale. They want to send him to reform school."

"Why?"

"Because he had some kind of beef. You would know all about it if you went to the meetings like you're supposed to."

"I'm too busy for that shit. Or too lazy."

He chuckled in spite of himself. "Well, Mrs. Tunnicliffe wants to see you."

Once inside her office, I said, "I understand you want a with me."

"Where have you been hiding, Francis? It's like I never see you around."

"Not hiding, just busy with other things."

"Well, being student-body president means you have certain commitments and responsibilities. Now, Mac Yale got into some trouble and ended up before us. If you had been there, he would have felt more comfortable and confident about dealing with the administration. He says he admires and envies you a great deal."

"I really don't want the job. I don't want anyone admiring and envying me. I want Mack and everyone else to admire and envy themselves."

"Well," she said, "the fact is that you have the job and are in a position to be of help to Mack Yale."

"What can I do for him?"

"Be his friend. Everyone wants and needs a friend. He would confide in you; he would say,

'Francis, my life is pretty bad and here's why…' That way, we would have a pretty good idea of how to help him."

I nodded. "O.K., I'll be his friend. Everyone else seems to want my friendship, so I guess I can take on one more."

Chapter 7

"Did you see her?" Amnon asked me.

"Yes," I replied.

"And…?"

"She wants me to hang out with Mac and find out what's bugging him, then report back to her."

"How do you feel about that?"

I just shrugged.

"She wants you to do this," Amnon said, "because you're a leader at this school. You have everyone's respect."

"How nice for me."

"I'm going to meet Clark for a pop. Want to join us?"

"Can't do it. I have a class this period."

"Have fun." He walked away.

I headed down the hallway, and just as I got to my

destination, I saw Yael exit the room.

"Oh, you."

I snarled. "Yes, me." Then, "What's your problem, little girl?"

She shrugged. "No problem here, little boy. It's just that you're mean and hard, and I don't like those kinds of people."

"Well, I don't like ugly little spoiled brats, but I try to be nice to you anyway."

Eyes blazing, she moved in to slap me across the face and almost succeeded, but I caught her wrist. After we exchanged dirty looks for a few moments, I let her go.

"Don't do that again," I told her. "It shows weakness of character."

She blushed and said, "I suppose I've never given you a chance."

"Why not?"

"Because of Anya. I knew she was attracted to you and you sort of came between us."

Women are nuts, I said to myself.

Chapter 8

Someone grabbed me by the arm. I looked over and saw Amnon. "Right now," he said, "Mac is in the ifc waiting to see Mrs. Tunnicliffe. If you wanted to, you could go there right now and make friends with him. That way, you could start having confidential conversations with him."

"Is that her idea?"

"Yes."

"I'm due in Spanish class. I can't skip out."

"Francis, Mac Yale is more important than Spanish class."

Down at the office, I said to Mac, "Hey, guy! How's it goin', eh?"

"I need to see Mrs. Tunnicliffe," he said, all hangdog. "I'm in trouble. Maybe they'll lock me up."

I sat down next to him. "Too bad, eh? Anything I can do to help?"

"I doubt it," he said, fighting back tears.

"Tell me what's wrong. I'm Francis Stone. I'm the student-body president and King Shit around here. You got a problem, you come to me. Simple as that."

He just shrugged. "I wanted a job for the summer. There aren't many opportunities for Native boys like me. I was thinking of shining shoes—"

I brightened up. "That's what I did when I lived at the orphanage!"

"Well, I didn't get to be a shine boy because I'm a Native and boys like me don't get any opportunities, even the bad ones. So I figure I'll just drop out of school. I'll probably end up in the joint."

"I have a few ideas on how I can help you improve your life," I lied. "Let me speak to Mrs. Tunnicliffe and find out what she thinks."

I went inside to meet with her. She said, "I think if you made him part of your class activities, it would help him because he admires you so much. You should also invite him to join your clique—you have a few of them, don't you?—and that would boost his self-esteem."

"If I appoint him to something I need the

160

approval of student council."

She smiled. "I can put that through."

I nodded. "I'll get started on his, uh, rehabilitation."

"But don't tell him this was my idea."

"Whatever you say. You're the boss."

Chapter 9

I got Mac a job as a cashier at the school's cafeteria and put him to work as the accountant of one of the school's clubs. A conscientious cashier and bookkeeper, he told me he was grateful for the salary and extra credit he received in compensation for his labors. His grades and attendance improved a great deal. I sometimes went out of my way to check him out and ask him if everything was O.K.; he seemed reasonably content most of the time.

By and by, election time approached. I definitely did not want to run again; I was much too busy with other things. At school, I had sports and whatnot to eat up my free time. Outside of school, I had my family and friends to take turn kissing my butt. I liked thinking that I was the most important person in all of humankind.

One afternoon, we—Tina, Steve, Amnon, and I—went to Tina's to hang out. I sat in the place of honor, which was the big recliner her father liked, and everyone sat surrounding me. I spoke first.

"I don't want to run again. I have other things to do that mean much more to me."

"You should run again because you would win easily," said Steve.

"Fuck that noise," I retorted. "The job is a hassle and I don't want to do it any longer."

"How do you know the job is a hassle?" Amnon asked. "Tina has been doing it for you."

"If Tina has any *kvetches*," I said, "she'll make them herself." I looked at her. "Well…?"

She smiled. "No *kvetches* here."

"Well, there it is," I said to Amnon. "If you clowns think it's such a great gig, *you* should run in the next election."

Amnon shook his head. "No can do here. I have so much to do with Mrs. Tunnicliffe—"

"O.K., then quit your bitching! And Tina, how about it?"

"Tina?" Amnon cried out. "No girl has ever been

class president."

"There's a first time for everything," I said.

Tina shook her head. "They would never elect me, but Steve? Yeah, he would win."

We looked at him. He smiled. He was a handsome kid. "O.K., I'll do it, but on one condition."

"Which is…?" I asked.

"That Tina runs with me."

"Done," I said.

The next day Mrs. Tunnicliffe approached me in the hallway. "They tell me you're not running."

I smirked. "I think Oliver Johnson Secondary will survive with out having me as president."

"But I thought you changed your mind after our conversation."

"No, ma'am."

"What about those things you could do for Mac?"

"Mac is doing them for himself."

"I'm thinking that I may have been wrong about you," she said.

"Could be you were," I replied.

"Then that's a shame. I liked you." She went into her office.

Clark and Tina won easily, and I began spending less time with my old clique. Due to my athletic abilities I started hanging out with the older students, the upperclassmen. They considered me their friend and I theirs. I spent little time with the students my own age because I felt much older and more sophisticated by then.

I reduced my dates with Tina and started seeing older girls. They had bigger breasts and let me feel them up.

One day Clark caught up with me. "Hey!" he said.

"Hey yourself!" I said back.

"You been avoiding us?"

"No, just busy living life and chasing my dreams."

"Tina says you haven't been calling or dating her."

"Too bad for Tina."

"But—"

"Tina and I are not married," I told him.

He got up in my face. "I've been waiting for you to say that."

"Well, it's the truth."

"You've been neglecting us," he said, his eyes narrowing. "Don't do that. Remember who your friends are." He walked away.

I shrugged and tried to forget about what he had just said. Still, I went by Tina's that evening to say hello and remind her that we still belonged to the same clique. I knocked on her door and she said, "Hey, Francis, come in."

We went into her parlor; Clark and Amnon were already there. I wondered why they were present but I was careful not to show any surprise when I saw them there.

"How's it goin', eh?" I said to those assembled.

"Why, it's Mr. Big Man on Campus!" Amnon exclaimed. "How kind of you to condescend to spend some time with us!"

"Oh, fuck off," I retorted.

"So, Francis," Clark said, "why did you come here?"

"I came here to see Tina, just like you."

"We're here to discuss school business," said Amnon.

"Well, I'm here for social reasons," I said. "When you're done with the school business, you can piss off and I'll visit with Tina." I grabbed a magazine and sat down to read it. "Where are your mum and dad?"

"Gone to Granny's," said Tina. "She's feeling poorly."

"Hard luck. Nothing serious, I hope."

"Just a cold."

"She'll be fine." Amnon said, "Well, our business is over. We'll be going now."

"What's your hurry?' I asked.

"Yeah. I'll put on the radio," Tina said. "Find a good music station. We can dance."

Soon they left. I held out my arms to her and said, "Give Daddy a kiss."

She did as told, and when we came up for air I said, "Yummy!"

"That was our first time in a little while," she said.

"I had forgotten how good it felt. Otherwise I would have come by more often."

"Don't lie, Francis," she said. "You don't have to

168

lie to me. Anyway, I don't like liars."

"O.K., never again," I lied.

Chapter 10

I was eating lunch one day when Amnon plopped down next to me. "Hey, Francis," he said. "How's it goin', eh?"

"You tell me," I retorted.

"Everyone's saying you don't want to run for re-election because you think you're better than everyone else."

"Everyone can kiss my ass."

"Mrs. Tunnicliffe is disappointed in you, too."

"She can kiss my ass, too."

"That's the wrong attitude. What's your problem, anyway?"

"No problem here." I had bought a large bottle of milk and drank down half of it. I wiped my lips with the back of my free hand. "I'm getting a little sick of the bullshit she hands out all the time about helping the students. She doesn't want to help the students—she wants the students to help each other." Then, "Why don't you have some lunch?"

"Not hungry. I came down here to talk to you. Mrs. Tunnicliffe wants you to come back upstairs and help her with some things. She says you've been a big help to her."

I shook my head and stood up. "Not interested."

"As you wish. But I think you're making a big mistake."

I shrugged. "I have a Ph.D. in fucking up."

After lunch, I went across the street and sat on a bench. Half a dozen other benches sat vacant. I took a deep breath of April air and smiled. Vancouver could be the most charming of places on a good day. I heard the school bell ring and decided to skip out. Sometimes school just was not my thing.

A bevy of girls emerged from the school. One of them was Tina. She headed in my direction. I looked away, hoping she wouldn't see me, but she did. She said something to the other girls and walked over to my bench. I hoped she wouldn't sit with me, but she did.

"Hey, Francis," she said with a big dimpled smile. Her smile always got me. It said, 'I'm sorry if I did anything wrong. I meant well.'

"Hello, Tina," I said.

"I'm sure you have a class right now. Skipping out, eh?"

"Pretty much."

"Mind if I sit with you?"

I shrugged. "It's a free country."

She sat at the other end of the bench. "You've changed in the past year, Francis."

"Well, I've tried."

"I don't mean that in a good way. You've grown cold and distant."

Yael had said the same thing. "I've always been that way. I was born that way."

"Francis, how come you've stopped coming by to see me?"

"I've been so busy with so many things. Everyone has been pulling me in every direction..."

"You were busy before and you always made time for us."

"You seem to have been hanging out with Clark a

lot. I guess you haven't been lonely."

"I started doing that only because you weren't around." Then, "I thought you loved me."

I threw out my hands. "I *did* love you. I *do* love you."

She shook her head. "Go away. Leave me alone."

I swore under my breath and headed back to school.

Chapter 11

The family was getting ready for dinner when I got home. "Hello, everyone," I said.

"Francis!" exclaimed my aunt. "We were starting to wonder where you'd gone. Hurry up and wash."

I frowned; she, the gentlest creature alive, sounded almost harsh. She wrinkled her little features into a mass of worry lines. "You know me, Auntie," I said, in a lame effort at levity. "I'm never one to miss a meal."

The girls giggled. "He's right, Mum," said Esther. "That boy is never late for meals."

I went into the parlor and discovered my uncle sitting alone, staring out the window. "You surprised me," I said to him. "I thought you weren't home yet."

"Hello, Francis," he said. "I came home early. I was tired."

"We're ready to eat," I said. "Let's go."

"I'm not hungry." Then, "You'll find out sooner or

later. I have tuberculosis. The doctors want me to move to Arizona."

Well, that was one more thing for me to worry about.

Chapter 12

I woke up late for school and had to run. I barely made it to my first class. Later on I saw Steve. We made small talk for a few minutes; after that I saw Yael in the lunchroom. I sat down next to her and said, "How's it goin', eh?"

"I'm busy," she said. "Got tests to ace, good grades to make."

"More power to ya."

"How come you haven't been hanging out with us lately? Amnon says he doesn't see you around much. You two didn't punch it out or anything, did you?"

I chuckled. "Not yet. We just have different things to do."

"Well, drop by sometime—if you can pencil us in." She got up and left.

I sat there for a while and gazed around the lunchroom. The place looked different to me—or maybe I was looking at it differently because I believed I would be moving away soon.

Back at home, I went into the parlor. My aunt sat there reading the newspaper. "This is the first time today that I've had some time to myself."

"When are we going to leave? I wonder if I'll like Arizona."

"We have to get things taken care of here first. Your uncle has to sell off his business and we'll have to check out schools down there for you and the girls. Money will be very, very tight. Your uncle will really have to take it easy and not exert himself."

"I'm sure I can get a job."

"We're hoping that won't be necessary. We want you to go to college and have a career that's worthy of you. Have you thought about what you would like to do?"

"Not often," I said.

"I think you would be happy as a doctor or lawyer."

"Well, that's for another day. Did the doctor say

how bad his condition is?"

"It could be much worse. Tuberculosis isn't the death sentence that cancer is. The doctor says he'll improve soon."

"I hope he's right."

"You know, Francis, you seem very precocious—quite mature for your age."

I smiled.

Then my uncle entered the room. My aunt looked up at him, beaming. "How did it go?"

He smiled. "It went all right. I met with some people to see about selling off my assets and they were going to give me a very reasonable price. We'll be able to get along O.K. on that money for a while. But there's a problem: When I went to the provincial office to tell them I was leaving British Columbia, they asked about Francis and I told them the truth. They said we couldn't take him with us."

"What?" I exclaimed.

He looked at me. "It seems that there's a rule with the orphanage that if a family adopts a child and that family has a member who develops a communicable disease, the adopted child must return to the orphanage. You may have to go back there for a while. I don't know for sure. I'll see my lawyer tomorrow and maybe he can fix things. He's pretty good about doing what I want him to do."

I shook my head. "I won't go back to that awful place."

"Maybe you won't have to," my uncle said.

We got busy fast. May arrived and we made tentative arrangements to move into a house near Phoenix. My aunt began some very early packing. The dreary, gray, cool Vancouver days and nights got warmer, or at least milder. As I helped my aunt with this and that, we all jabbered with the utmost excitement about our new life in Arizona and all the adventures we would have there.

At about two in the afternoon, my uncle came in, looking exhausted and forlorn. He sat down and my aunt made him some tea, which he sipped slowly.

"Francis, sit down," he said to me.

I nodded and sat on the sofa next to my aunt.

"No bad news, I hope," I said.

He sighed. "I may as well just say this bluntly: You won't be able to move to Arizona with us."

"But—"

He held up a hand, to shush me. "As you know, I met with my lawyer so that we could get an exemption for you or something, but he said his hands are tied because the law is what it is. You will have to return to the orphanage till you're eighteen, at which time you will be free to join us out West."

I swallowed hard, wanting desperately to throw a temper tantrum but making damn sure I did no such thing. I had convinced myself that I would be going to Arizona with them. I felt devastated.

My aunt looked at me and spoke, her voice soft and empathic. "Francis, in some ways this news is not altogether a bad thing. You'll be able to finish school here. You'll be among your friends, and you *know* how much everyone here admires and respects you. Soon you will graduate from high school and then you'll be able to join us. You can go to college out there—they have many fine universities, as I'm sure you're aware. Best thing for us to do is go ahead and move to Arizona and tell ourselves—and each other—that you're in college out here and will rejoin us once you graduate."

I shook my head with some vehemence. "I don't *want* to pretend! I don't want to stay here! I want to be with you!"

"And we want you to be with us," said my aunt. "This matter is difficult for all of us. But as the lawyer said, the law is the law and our hands are tied."

I did not cry, but tears streamed down my face and I wiped them away. I looked at my aunt and tears streamed down her face, too. My uncle seemed on the verge of losing his composure. I stood, wiped more tears from my cheeks and raced into my bedroom. I slammed the door, threw myself onto my bed and burst into tears.

I heard a knock on the door. Then I heard my aunt say, "Don't go in there. If anyone should do it, it's me. He's acting like a little kid whose parents have just said, 'Go away. You're not welcome here anymore.'"

"We'll just leave him alone," said Uncle Daniel. "He's a grown man now. He'll just learn to deal with this whole situation in his own way."

I lay there sniffling, feeling very flattered by what he had said about my being a "grown man." Maybe I was, but at that particular moment I was doing a great imitation of a two-year-old who was acting out because he didn't get his way.

I took a deep breath and got out of bed. I washed my face and went into the kitchen to join my aunt and uncle. We had a cup of tea and I felt a bit better. I promised myself that I would do my best to be the "grown man" my aunt and uncle thought I was. I also promised myself I would never indulge in self-pity again.

Chapter 13

On May 13, 1927, it was back-to-the-orphanage time. My uncle helped me load his car with my stuff.

"Ready to go?" he asked.

I nodded. "Let's do it."

"I thought we could avoid this," he said as we drove along. If that was an apology, it was unnecessary. He had been wonderful to me.

When we got there, he and I shook hands with Brother Lawrence. "Welcome back, Francis," he said.

Back in my old room, I immediately saw one of the kids from before—John Driver. He had grown; he was now nearly my height.

"You're back, eh?" he said.

"'Fraid so," I replied.

After saying goodbye to my uncle I told Brother Lawrence I was going to go for a brief walk. Instead, I withdrew money from my bank account and hurried over to the train station. I bought a ticket to Seattle.

Interlude

TINA

As she listened to Amnon speak, she noted that he could scarcely keep his eyes open. She wished he would shut up and go to bed. This was one of those evenings when she sat and wondered what awaited her in life. She hoped, but was not entirely sure, that there would be more good than bad.

On Monday at school, she had just entered the building when a messenger arrived to collect and deliver her to Mrs. Tunnicliffe's office. She went upstairs with her escort, wondering what was so important that it couldn't wait till later. Nobody sat in the outer office, so she went right inside.

Mrs. Tunnicliffe sat at her desk. An unfamiliar man sat in front of her, and Amnon and Clark were also present. Both boys immediately looked at her, their faces strained with worry.

"Brother Lawrence," said Mrs. Tunnicliffe as she stood, "this is Tina Lundquist. I told you about her. Tina, this is Brother Lawrence from St. Anthony's orphanage."

"Hello, Brother," said Tina, wondering why she had been invited to this little meeting.

"Tina," he said, "have you seen or heard from Francis Stine in the past few days?"

She shook her head. "Is anything wrong?"

"Well, yes. He was supposed to move back in with us until age eighteen but he has run away instead."

"I know he has family," she said. "Maybe he's with them."

"No. We sent them a telegram and they said he wasn't there."

"Didn't he say anything to anyone?" Mrrs. Tunnicliffe said to no one in particular.

Tina collapsed into a chair and began to weep.

"Don't cry," said Steve. "It could be that he wanted to go off and be alone for a while so he could get his head together."

"But maybe he's hurt or sick or already dead," she said between sobs.

Clark put his hand on her shoulder. "Don't worry about him, Tina. He's wise beyond his years. He knows how to take care of himself."

She looked up at him with tear-stained cheeks. "*Think* so?"

"I *know* so."

This was the first time she knew how Clark felt about her. She burst into tears again—for herself, Francis and Steve.

She and Clark had become inseparable after that. They spoke little of Francis for the longest time until that evening a short time before their wedding.

They had had dinner at Steve's parents' house. Clark had been recently licensed as an attorney in British Columbia and would soon start working in the Crown prosecutor's office. They sat side by side in the living room and watched the fireplace as it crackled and roared.

"What's on your mind, sweetness?" Clark murmured, giving her hand a tiny squeeze.

She kept her gaze on the fire. "Not much."

"You were so quiet, I thought maybe you had forgotten I was here."

"Impossible. You're the man I love. It's just that I've been spending some time these days thinking back on my life as a single lady before I become a married lady."

"I don't want you to be unhappy, ever. My goal is to see to it that Mrs. Clark Rutledge never has an unhappy moment in her life."

"Well, everyone has a few unhappy moments. It's just a part of life." Then, "I love you, Steve."

"And I love you, Tina."

They were married at noon at St. Bart's Church, just as their wedding invitations said they would be.

"Remember Francis Stone?" Amnon was saying as they continued staring at the fireplace. "I always looked at him and thought, 'I want to be Francis when I grow up.'"

190

Tina nodded and sipped her wine. "He was someone different. He was big, tough, handsome, smart. Plus, there was something dangerous about him. He was a bad boy, and many girls, myself included, found him very attractive." She smiled at her fiancé and he smiled back. Enough time had passed; they could speak of these things now, even laugh about them.

"But there was always something about him that made you question his sincerity. He would lie to you just to get you to do whatever he wanted you to do."

"Yes," said Tina, "that's what it was." Then, as if wanting to change the subject, she said, "Shall we have coffee in the living room?"

PART THREE

Chapter 1

I woke up the next morning in an unfamiliar room. After wasting a few minutes staring at the ceiling, I looked around my room and realized I was in Seattle. I hadn't meant to bugger off that way and tried to talk myself into returning to Vancouver. When that failed, I washed my face in the rusted-out little basin and got dressed. As I did so, I wondered what everyone was doing back home. When I hadn't shown up on time, Brother Lawrence surely contacted my aunt and uncle, who in turn had called the Vancouver police. The cops up there would figure out soon enough that I had bought a ticket for Seattle. I knew better than to think I could stay off the radar screen for very long, so I resolved to check out of my room right away and get lost in the Emerald City.

Downstairs, I handed my key to the desk clerk and told him I was checking out. He just nodded and went back to reading the Seattle *Chronicle*. I bought myself a copy of the *Chronicle* at a newsstand and went into a café for breakfast—scrambled eggs, toast, juice and coffee—that cost me thirty cents, which was more than I wanted to pay. As I ate I looked through the HELP WANTED section for jobs I might be considered for. I marked them with a pencil and finished eating.

By lunchtime I had pursued some of those leads but remained unemployed. Occasionally I got lost on the streets of Seattle but each time I stopped to ask for directions the passerby gave me accurate information with a smile. Back in Vancouver, the person giving me directions would practically smirk at my ignorance.

I decided that I should find somewhere to sleep that night before I did anything else. I opened my newspaper again and checked out the ROOMS FOR RENT section; all of the accommodations seemed to be located in the same seedy part of town, which should not have surprised me. I boarded a trolley and headed out that way. When I got off, most of the buildings were dreary old stone edifices with handwritten VACANCY signs. Most of those lodging places looked unfit for human habitation. I looked at one after another till I found one that seemed less dreadful than the others. I rang the bell but no one answered. I rang it again and still got no response. I shrugged and started to walk away when I heard the door open and an old woman wearing a bathrobe appeared.

"Why did you ring the bell?" she shouted. "I was taking a nap."

"You have a sign in the window," I replied. "I need a place to stay."

"Well, you can't stay here. Someone else got the room yesterday. I forgot all about that sign."

"Oh, O.K." I started to walk away.

"You're Canadian, aren't you?"

"Yes," I told her, "I am a Canadian in search of a room to live in. Do you have any idea where I might find one?"

"I like Canadians. Maybe I have a room for you after all. Come inside."

Presently we stood in the middle of a large room that contained sofas, chairs and a grand piano.

"Yuck! Stinks in here, eh?" the woman said. She smirked. "Isn't 'eh' what you Canadians say? Did I just make you homesick? Why did you come down to the States, anyway?"

I shrugged. "Boredom, I guess."

"Let's sit and chat."

The woman sat on the sofa and I took the chair nearest her. "So," she said, "how old are you?"

"Nineteen," I lied.

"And you left Canada out of boredom."

"Yes…and at this moment what I really, really need is a room to rent. Can you help me?"

"You left Canada out of boredom. Is that the truth, or did you just knock up some Canadian girl and run off?"

"No such thing."

"Are the cops up there after you?"

Well, she wasn't as dumb as I'd thought. As soon as Brother Lawrence called the Vancouver police, the Seattle police would catch up with me.

"Yeah," she said, "the cops are after you. What are you going to do here in Seattle?"

"Get a place to stay and look for a job."

"Got a green card? I'll bet you don't. Good luck finding a job in the States when you don't have a green card."

"Well," I said, getting up, "it's been very interesting meeting you."

"Sit still." She took a long hard look at me. "I like you, believe it or not. You're a rough, tough character. Maybe I have a job for you."

"That right, eh? Doin' what?" I hoped she wouldn't suggest pimping or peddling dope.

"You can see what kind of place I run here, can't you?"

I nodded. "We have these same kinds of places up in Vancouver."

"Well, the people who live here are mostly men and when they get a few beers in them, they sometimes don't mind their manners. I need a big, mean-looking guy who can keep the Neanderthals in line. These men are unruly only when they're drunk, and then they're easy enough to handle. I would also need you to come to the store with me because I'm not getting any younger. Thirty dollars a week plus room and board. Interested?"

"Not exactly what I had in mind."

She smiled. "I can guarantee you that I'm making you the best offer you will get in Seattle. Also, we'll pretend you aren't a foreigner without a green card."

"I don't want to pimp."

"Did I say pimping? No, I don't believe I did."

I nodded. "When do I start?"

"Immediately. Keep your hands of the girls when you're in public...but if you choose to do some discreet groping, nobody will mind."

"I hear you."

She leaned forward, as if confiding in me. "You do your job and keep your yap shut and I promise the cops won't know you're here."

I smiled and chuckled. "Hey, I like that."

"What's your name?"

"Francis Stone. What do I call you?"

"Just call me Mama."

Chapter 2

"I'm glad you accepted my offer," said Mama. She went to one end of the room and screamed, "Angel! Angel!" She asked me, "Where's your stuff?"

"Don't have any," I told her.

"No luggage?"

"None."

She sighed. "Just like a young person, running off without any luggage. I'll bet you don't have any money, either."

I shrugged, thinking of the $185 in my pocket.

"That won't do," she said. "When we go out shopping this afternoon, I'll get you all fixed up with some suits and colorful shirts. Of course, I'll deduct it from your salary."

Just then a big black girl lumbered into the room. "Hello, Mama."

"My grandson here just got in from Vancouver. Show him the empty room."

The black girl frowned at me.

"You got a problem, honey bunch? I said he's my grandson from Canada and I want you to show him to the room. Now, which part of what I just said did you fail to understand?"

The girl pouted. "I knowed you for six years, Mama, and you ain't said one word 'bout havin' no gran'sons."

Mama shook her head and said to me, "That's niggers for you. They don't mind sassin' you even if you put 'em to work and feed 'em."

The black girl swallowed hard and looked at the floor. "Whatever you say, Miz Mama."

Mama threw back her head and laughed. "Well, he don't mean shit to me. I never saw him before today. But if I say he's my kin, that's good enough for you." She turned to me and said, "This is Angel. You can't bullshit her. Can we, Angel?"

The big girl giggled. "No, Mama, you cain't bullshit Angel."

"Well, then, go show him to his room. Then clean

202

up this room! It stinks! Then bring me some breakfast. Are you hungry, Francis?"

"No, Mama."

"All right, Francis. Go to your room. Give me an hour to eat. Then we'll go do some shopping." She walked away.

I followed Angel upstairs to my room. it contained a single bed, small desk and wash basin. "It ain' much," said Angel, "but it's cheap. Toilet's down the hall. Mama's room is across the hall an' mine is downstairs. All the girls be on the same flo'." She eyeballed me. "You sure you from Canada?"

"Yes."

"But you no relative of Mama?"

"I just met her."

She shrugged and left. I closed the door behind her. I removed my coat and tossed it onto a chair. Then I flopped onto the bed and stared at the ceiling, feeling tired yet restless. I closed my eyes, wishing to take a nap, but my mind was racing. I got up, went to the window, looked out at nothing for several long minutes, then returned to the bed and sprawled out on it.

That old woman who called herself Mama was a pain in my butt but she was right: I would never be discovered by the cops down here. As soon as things got nice and quiet I could rejoin my family. I wondered how they were doing. The old woman called Mama told me I was a tough guy. Well, I supposed I was that.

I began to fall asleep, but then Mama came in, looking like any other lady. We needed to go shopping together. I opened my eyes and got up.

"Time to do some shopping, Francis," she said.

I nodded. "Let's do it."

First we went to a butcher's shop, then a grocery store. Mama paid cash for her purchases and had them delivered. Our third stop was a tailor's shop.

A short, dapper Jewish man came up to us and said, "How may I help you?"

"I'm looking for some good secondhand suits," Mama told him.

"You came to the right place!" he exclaimed. "You want secondhand suits? I got them. Only thing is, mine don't look used—they look new."

"That's what I like to hear," Mama said. "I want

one or two for my grandson here."

We looked through what he had till she found one she liked. "Try it on," she said to me.

"Not that one, lady!" said the haberdasher. "That one is the best I got. I was saving it for myself." Nevertheless, he took it off the rack and smoothed it out so I could try it on. The suit was a gray pinstriped garment. It felt a bit too big in the shoulders.

"Perfect fit—almost. Take it in just a little bit in the shoulders," said the man.

"What's the price?" asked Mama.

"For you, twelve-fifty."

"I'll give you nine."

"Sold." Then, "I didn't want to sell this suit, but it's yours now. I'll take it in a little and it'll be fine."

"Pad the shoulders. I want him to look bigger than he is."

"Done. You're the boss."

Fifteen minutes later, I tried on the whole suit. Mama was right—the shoulders were broader and I looked more intimidating. I had to fight to keep from smirking. "Looks good, eh, Mama?"

The tailor wrapped up our purchase and we left.

We got home at six o'clock. I wondered what the rest of the people in the house were like. Mama knocked on the door and Angel let us in.

"Francis," said Mama, "we have dinner at six-thirty. Don't be late."

"I'm never late for dinner," I told her.

Chapter 3

I heard the ring of a bell and assumed that dinner was ready. I went downstairs and heard many voices, the loudest of which belonged to Mama. I ran a hand through my hair and went in to join them.

The chattering stopped and all faces turned to appraise me. I wasn't altogether sure what they thought of me but I supposed it really didn't matter— I wasn't there for their amusement. Everyone was already seated; I saw one vacant seat next to Mama so I went over and sat down.

"Help yourself, Francis," Mama said. "I'm sure you must be hungry."

I nodded and helped myself. Mama said, "This is Francis Stone. He's going to work here and help us keep things nice and tidy." She reached under the table, pulled out a bottle of vodka, drank down half of it as if guzzling water. Then she introduced me to each of the girls. I nodded and smiled at each of them, observing that all seemed to be between twenty-five and forty years old. They all wore kimonos or bathrobes and most wore garish, amateurishly applied makeup. They looked to me like a bunch of whores. That was O.K.; I had already met my share of such women.

Angel seemed to be the leader of the pack, to the extent that this pack had a leader. A big human being, she had long, thick arms, much belly fat, three chins, a broad backside and shiny blonde hair. As she checked me out, I just kept eating, pretending to be oblivious to her attention. Then she said, "Mama, how come you think we need this wimpy boy as a bouncer? He ain't no bigger'n a doodle bug. We don't need no boy aroun' here, we need a *man*." She kept on looking at me, clearly wanting me to make some sort of retort. But I just kept on eating.

Mama just laughed and drank some more booze.

Angel stood up, taking our silence as permission for her to run her bog mouth some more. "He just a little boy. Look at him! He look like he about to cry!

Get him out of here 'fore he busts out bawlin'!"

I put down my utensils and looked up at her. She must have been five-ten and weighed one-eighty. The others girls stared at her, waiting to do whatever she wanted them to.

What she did next was to pinch my cheek and say, "Jes' a li'l baby. Run on home to Mum, li'l baby."

When I said and did nothing, Angel grinned and said, "You gonna let me treat you that way, li'l baby?"

Without saying a word, I reached over and smacked in across the face with the back of my hand. She sprawled backwards, lost her footing and let out a whimper as blood trickled from her mouth.

"You need to mind your manners," I said as I kept on eating. I could see her staring at me, wobbling as she stood, unsure of what, if anything, she should say or do next. She feared me. Many people had feared me during my young life. I kind of liked it.

Mama laughed. "I told you not to hassle him! I told you to show him some respect!"

Angel sat down and continued eating. The other girls kept eating, too. One by one they finished up and left the table. Presently only Mama and I remained. The old woman was mostly shitfaced. "Angel is getting really fat," she said. "Soon the men won't want to boff her." Then, "Welcome to your new home, Francis."

At close to eight o'clock the girls came downstairs to sit in the parlor and wait for the horny men to arrive. The females all wore satin dresses and had done their makeup and hair with much care. It didn't take me long to observe that those ladies were going commando. Angel sat with the others, chatting a bit with them and offering me an impersonal little smile, as if our confrontation earlier hadn't happened. They often called her Big Angel, to tell her apart from Angel the black maid. Soon Mary the servant appeared, dressed up for the evening but not at all like a whore. She sat at the piano and played bluesy tunes—that was her job for the evening.

From somewhere else in the big house Mama appeared—cold sober. How could that be? I asked myself. When we left the dinner table she was falling-down drunk. Her hair was neat and tidy and she wore a sensible beige outfit. Mama became whoever she needed to be as that need arose, I supposed.

She told me, "Remember—get the money at the first opportunity. Five dollars per customer—twenty-five if he wants to spend the night. Get the money before he lays a finger on her. Stay out in the hallway so everyone will know you're the bouncer; I'll take care of whatever business comes up in other parts of the house." She walked away. I watched her return with some bottles of liquor and empty glasses, which she placed on the fireplace. The girls all shifted in their seats and glanced at one another. Time to hustle the rubes and make some cash..

I looked through the peephole and saw a small man waiting at the door. He looked like an office clerk or haberdasher. "Is Mama in?" he asked. I opened the door and let him in. A regular visitor, he headed straight for the parlor. I could hear him saying hello to everyone, and presently he reappeared in the hallway with his arm around Angel, who gave me a smug little smile—all of those women were available to him and he chose her! He stuck a small wad of cash into my hand and I counted it—three dollars. I held up three fingers at Mama and she nodded.

"Go ahead," I said in my best tough-guy growl.

The doorbell rang again—another guy wanting some company. I let him in and he hurried into the parlor. Then others came in. I could hear laughter and the clink of glasses. The girls went upstairs with the men. Angel came downstairs with the little man and helped him with his coat.

"You be comin' by next week?" she asked him.

"Count on it!"

She went back into the parlor.

The night went on and on without any issues at all. The air stayed full with the sounds of laughter, glasses clinking, the melancholy notes of a bluesy piano tune, the flushing of toilets and creaking of doors.

At about three in the morning Mama came up to me. "Any cheapskates up there?"

"None."

"Then it's closing time."

I nodded and locked the door. We went into the kitchen and Mama opened the safe she kept in there.

"You should have three hundred fifty dollars," she told me. She held out a piece of paper and I took it. On it she had written each girl's name, how much business she had done that evening and how much she had charged. I counted the money and she counted it and I discovered that Mama was right.

After the money was in the safe, Mama said to me, "Want a drink?"

"No, thanks, Mama" I replied.

"Don't drink? Good for you. The shit will kill you," she told me as she downed a shot of gin.

I nodded.

"I never drink while I'm working," she added as she downed another shot.

"Good idea."

"You can go to sleep now, Francis," she said. "Your shift is over. You must be sleepy."

I did as told. In my bedroom, I pulled off my clothes and collapsed onto my bed. But I could not fall asleep. I stared for the longest time at nothing till my eyes ached from exhaustion and smoked a few cigarettes out of sheer restlessness.

Something was wrong, very wrong, inside of me.

This was the first time in my life that I could not fall asleep at will. Suddenly I feared everything and nothing—I feared *fear*. I cried softly into my pillow. *This wasn't supposed to be my life*, I thought through my tears as I pictured Mama and Mary and all the lonely men who had paid to come here.

I felt dirty, filthy, soiled by these awful people and their dirty business. I missed my uncle and aunt and cousins and Brother Lawrence and everyone else had known in Vancouver.

Why had I ever run away?

Chapter 4

I remained wide awake and vibrating with anxiety throughout that night. I watched the dull gleam of dawn illuminate the room. I got up, went over to the window and lit a cigarette. Outside the streets were bare except for a milkman and this or that guy on his way to work. As the streetlights began to flicker pout I filled my sink with water and splashed some on my face. I got dressed and entered the silent hallway. Presently I left the house altogether and walked across the street to the small park and sat down to have a cigarette. Nearby, birds chirped, a fountain sprayed water high into the air and a young sailor lay sprawled on a bench.

A beat cop entered the park and spoke to the sailor, who snatched up his white cap from the ground and skulked away. The cop made his way over to me and I wondered what we would say to each other, and if he would recognize my Canadian accent, assume I was a runaway and send me back to Vancouver. I realized I wouldn't mind that, and in truth would be only too happy to be sent home.

"Good morning, young fellow," he said to me.

"Good morning," I replied.

"You're up very early," he said.

I shrugged. "Couldn't sleep."

He nodded. "There's a lot of that going around. It's a very warm May." He had red hair, a ruddy complexion and blue eyes—quite an Irishman. "Do you live around here?"

"Yessir. My grandmother lives here. I've come to live with her. I'm from Vancouver."

He nodded. "Canada is a fine country." Then, "Well, I must be going now. Have a great day."

"You do the same." As I watched him walk away, I suddenly felt very drowsy, and a moment later I nodded off. But minutes later a barking dog woke me up. I checked my watch—a little after eight. I felt hungry. I wandered around the park for a few moments and exited from the other end. In the distance I saw some stores. I walked in that direction.

I stopped at the first restaurant I found and had breakfast. At about ten I returned to the house and Angel the servant let me in.

"How come you up so early?" she asked.

"I'm an early riser."

"You have your breakfast yet?"

"Yeah—at some joint down the street." I headed into the parlor. Angel had just finished cleaning up the place. I sat in the parlor and began reading the newspaper I had just bought. All the doors and windows were wide open to allow the morning air to freshen up the premises. With the doors wide open I could see whoever came down the stairs. About an hour passed; I could smell bacon frying; so could the others—they began coming down.

Big Angel, the first to come down for breakfast, looked at me through the corner of her eye and opened her mouth, closed it, then opened it again.

"You not mad at me about last night?" she asked.

"I'm not mad at you if you're not mad at me."

She smiled. "Oh, I'm not mad at you."

"Then we'll just forget about it, O.K.?"

She smiled again. "O.K., I can do that."

Presently Mama came down. She headed straight for the liquor cabinet. Then she said, "Francis, you're up early. Couldn't you sleep?"

"Just an early riser."

"Are you hungry?"

"I've already eaten."

She shrugged and went into the kitchen.

A woman named Megan came down last. She was already fully dressed in a gray outfit and she wore a small gold cross around her neck. The others had come down in wraps, robes and whatnot.

"Good morning," she said to me.

"Hello."

"Had breakfast?"

"Yep."

She did a little dance for me. "Ooh, I feel good this mornin'. Thought I might even wanna go to Mass. Wanna join me?"

"No." I rolled my eyes. How could anyone with her lifestyle go to Mass? What could she say to Him that He would care to hear?

"You should come with me. Be good for you."

"Piss off."

She laughed and walked out the door.

Mama came in. "What's eating Megan? Besides the customers, I mean." She laughed at her own cleverness.

"She wanted me to go to Mass with her but I said no."

"Oh. Megan believes that she can be a whore all night and a good Catholic during the day and that will get her into heaven. Are you Catholic?"

"No."

She sipped at her drink. "Say, I think I heard someone crying in their sleep last night."

"Wasn't me," I said, hoping like hell I was right.

Chapter 5

It took me till Thursday night before I could make any firm decision about what I was going to do. The preceding days had been relatively quiet; Mama and the others had accepted me as part of their family, as it were—I had my place, they had theirs. We mostly respected each other's privacy. In my most private moments I wondered if I was pimping in this Seattle brothel and just lying to myself about it. I suppose I was ambivalent about what I wanted in life.

On Thursday afternoon I sat and smoked in the parlor as Seattle rain pounded the rooftop. Dammit, I thought, this city is as wet as Vancouver. Mama had gone to the picture show with one of the girls. I had seen that movie the day before and slept through most of it. I woke up feeling refreshed but bored so I left the picture house and crossed the street to buy a

Coke. I passed a Navy recruiting station and gazed at a poster inside on an exotic faraway island. I dreamed for a moment of faraway islands and beautiful women but then dismissed the idea and moved on.

I put down the newspaper and sighed. Today I had the blues in a big way. Angel didn't help my low mood much when she came in and started playing sad, sad songs. I got to thinking about Vancouver, family and friends.

"Angel," I said, "would you do me a big favor?"

"What you want, boss?"

"Quit playing that damned piano."

She got up and left the room.

"What's your problem, Francis?" asked Megan as she walked into the parlor in her black satin gown and gold cross and albino-white skin.

"No problem here," I muttered.

She sat on the arm of my chair and read the newspaper over my shoulder. "Why don't you fuck off?" I said.

"Why don't you?" she retorted in an even voice.

I said nothing.

"Why don't *you* fuck off? I mean, Francis, you're a nice Canadian boy who should not be working at a Seattle brothel. "

I got up and left the parlor. I headed for the front door, opened it and stood on the stoop, watching the Seattle downpour. In a moment Megan came out. I lit a cigarette.

"You can't go away," she said. "You have nowhere to go."

At once I felt better. She had just said the thing I knew was true but felt afraid to articulate. I smiled.

She frowned at me, then took a step back, like a boxer expecting to be hit. "You're mad as a hatter," she whispered. Then she disappeared back into the house.

I laughed again and took one last drag on my cigarette. Then I flicked the glowing butt into the Seattle rain.

The rest of the day went by very fast. I kept saying to myself, *I was afraid*. Yes, that's what it was, and each time I thought it. I started to understand why I had taken up Mama on her job offer. I wasn't as smart as I thought; the old lady had exploited me. First she had scared the shit out of me with her talk of calling the cops on me, and she continued to make the tacit threat of calling the cops on me if I stepped out of line. Well, I thought with a laugh, I'm not going to be afraid of anyone anymore.

I stood at the door that evening with a different attitude as I began to observe the tawdriness and shabbiness of the brothel, the girls' essential indifference to their customers and the utter falseness of it all.

One evening a sailor came in, went upstairs with Megan for an hour and came back down laughing. To me he said, "Aren't you a little young to be the bouncer?"

"This is just for now. I'm movin' on."

"Nice for you." He started for the exit.

"Wait!"

He turned around. "Yeah?"

"Is it true about the Navy? Seeing the world and getting an education and the rest of it?"

"You want to join up?"

"If they'll have me."

He smirked. "Oh, they will. And you'll be moving up in the world. Being a swabby is better than bing a brothel bouncer." He cackled and walked away. I watched him disappear.

Mama came up to me and said, "What were you talking to that swabby about?"

I shrugged. "He dropped his wallet and I gave it back to him."

She nodded. "You're very honest."

Chapter 6

At ten o'clock the next morning I sipped coffee in a restaurant and stared at the military recruiting station that would open at any moment. When the crew-cut Marine finally unlocked the doors, I went in and told him I wanted to enlist.

"Marines or Navy?" he asked me.

"Navy."

"Go sit over there."

I did as told. Soon the Navy recruiter came in, a young man with a bald head.

"Name?"

"Francis Stone."

"Address?"

I gave him the address of the best little whorehouse in the Pacific Northwest.

"Birthdate?"

"June six, Nineteen-oh-six."

"That means you're eighteen now. You'll need your parents' consent if you want to enlist."

"They're dead."

"Who's your guardian?"

"My grandmother. I live with her."

"She'll do. We'll mail her the consent forms."

Damn. I hadn't thought of that. Still, I felt quite sure that I could get to those documents before she knew they had arrived, then I could forge them and send them back and she would never be the wiser. He stood up and so did I.

"As soon as your grandmother signs those papers, bring them down here along with three days' worth of clothing. When you receive your physical examination, if you pass—as I'm sure you will—you will be sent to basic training."

"Good to know," I said.

He stuck out his hand and I shook it. "Congratulations," he said.

I walked back to the house, my head in the clouds.

Several days later, the letter arrived. Angel the servant always put the day's mail on the table in the parlor. The letter said UNITED STATES SELECTIVE SERVICE OFFICIAL BUSINESS. I looked this way and that, then slipped the letter into my jacket pocket. Up in my bedroom, I forget Mama's signature and put the letter back into my pocket.

My last night with Mama and the girls was very ordinary—just the usual thing. After the men left, Mama and I went into the kitchen with the wads of cash to count and put it all away. Afterwards we sat there and stared at each other for a while.

"You don't look sleepy," she said. "What's on your mind?"

"This is my last night here."

"Where will you go? What will you do?"

I just shrugged.

"Oh, so it's none of my business," she muttered. "What about the clothing I bought you?"

"Wear it yourself."

"I paid damn good money for that stuff!"

"I didn't force you to buy it for me. You insisted

on buying it for me."

"I'll give you a raise."

"Mo. I don't like the job."

"Look," she said. "Stick around and you'll make more money than you ever dreamed. You'll end up running this place. You'll be set for life."

"I don't like the job," I repeated.

"Go to hell!" she screamed.

I got up.

"Francis," she said, "don't go away mad."

"I'm just going away."

The next morning I was sworn into the United States Navy. "I pledge allegiance to the flag..."

Interlude

STEVE

"You know what, Steve?" Amnon was asking. "You've never told us how you met Francis."

Clark grinned. "I met you the same way you did—we were going to punch it out. Very soon we figured out that he couldn't kick my ass and I couldn't kick his. So we shook hands and became friends.

"That was a long time ago, of course. Back then I was attending a private school near the University of British Columbia. My dad came out there once for a visit. He was a wonderful guy—he told me what was on his mind, wanted my opinions on this and that and he always treated me with respect; he was never condescending to me.

"So he was saying to me, 'You see, Steve, in a couple of years I'm going to run for mayor...'

"I told him he would win, partly because I knew that the incumbent was someone the voters were getting sick of..

"Anyway, I soon transferred to St. Anthony's. I didn't like it; I was a child of privilege—handsome, smart, polite—and the school was filthy and the other kids were poor, dumb and ugly. I didn't necessarily consider myself inherently superior to them, but I certainly didn't feel part of the place the way I had felt at the private school I had transferred from."

He laughed at himself. "Maybe I *did* have a superiority complex but I tried to get over it. My father was a leader of men and I wanted to be one, too—someone who had the respect of admiration of everyone everywhere. I could see right away that Francis was someone who just naturally had that same quality that makes everyone pay attention to him and do as he said."

"But you didn't know he'd run off the way he did instead of going back to the orphanage," Amnon said.

"Well, I knew he hated the orphanage."

Tina said, "I hope we haven't seen the last of Francis. I hope we'll see him again, but I'm not sure how that will happen."

PART FOUR

Chapter 1

I stood there on the final day of 1931 and looked out at San Diego Bay, telling myself that the day sure felt cold; I had always thought that way down here the weather was always warm and sunny. I had my discharge papers in my pocket and my duffel bag lay at my feet.

I was glad to be a civilian again. I didn't necessarily think the Navy was a bad thing, but when they tell you all the time where to go and what to do, you stop being a grown, intelligent man and start being a robot. The military had been a decent enough place for me to bide my time before rejoining my family—certainly it had been better for me than the orphanage. Going from the orphanage to the Navy probably had been swapping one form of institutionalization, but now I was a free man and quite glad of it.

Navy life had mostly bored the hell out of me. I felt eager to see my aunt, uncle and cousins again, so I sent them a telegram saying I would contact them as soon as I reached Arizona.

The next day I received a message at my hotel room that my telegram could not be delivered because its recipient had moved. I went to the telegram office and walked up to the girl at the desk. I showed her what they had sent me saying my uncle had moved. "Are you sure about this? Maybe there has been a mistake."

"No, sir, there is no mistake, unfortunately," she said. Then, "How do you like being a civilian? I can tell by your haircut that you were in the service."

"I hated the Navy."

"But you're probably feeling a bit disoriented about your life right now."

"Very disoriented."

"Too bad about your telegram."

"Yeah, too bad." I added, "Thanks for your interest in my issues."

"I have a cousin in the Navy. I often wonder

238

how he feels about military life and what he'll do in civilian life."

"Yeah," I said, nodding. "You give it some thought."

"And what are you going to do?"

"Dunno. I guess something'll turn up."

"Jobs are hard to find these days."

"I've always gotten them when I've needed them."

"Speaking of jobs," she said, getting up, "it's quitting time for me. I need to go home and have dinner."

"Call home and tell them you're going to have dinner with very charming, recently discharged Navy man. I don't know this city very well and you could show me around."

She smiled. "I'm flattered by your interest, but I really should go home."

Like hell she did! She was just playing hard to get. "Please have dinner with me," I said to her. "You don't know how lonely a person gets, being a stranger in a strange town."

She nodded. "All right, Mr. Stone. But first I

have to call home and tell them I have other plans for this evening."

"Call me Francis."

"O.K., Francis; you can call me Ellen."

I sat there waiting while Ellen went into a phone booth and called home to tell them she would be eating with me, not them.

We went to some nightclub where they had a pretty popular show. We ate steaks and drank cocktails. I had never been much of a drinker, but on that evening I really didn't give a shit. I drank and danced and danced and drank. Soon I checked my watch and saw the time: one forty-five. We left the cabaret and got into a taxi.

"Where do you live?" I asked her.

"I can't go home like this," she said, swallowing a small alcoholic giggle. "My father would never forgive me."

"Where will you stay?"

"At a local hotel. That's what I do whenever I'm out partying late at night."

We went off to the hotel and she giggled. "What's funny?" I asked her.

"This. I feel ridiculous."

"That right, eh?" I put my arm around her and pulled her in. I kissed her. "Still feel ridiculous?"

"You sure can kiss."

"I have many talents. I am a very talented person."

Just then she pushed me away. "The hotel! We're here!" she smoothed out her clothes and climbed out of the car. I followed her.

"Let's go in," I said.

She shook her head. "No. We better just say goodnight out here."

I nearly laughed. Francis Stone didn't spend his money on a woman just so she could say goodnight and walk away. I said, "I'm going to stay here, too," and marched into the lobby.

Once I got to my room, I felt happy that I'd spent the evening with a pretty young lady and eager to get a good night's sleep. Presently I heard a knock on my door so I opened it.

"Want some company?" asked Ellen.

"Come in. I didn't thank you for the good time we had."

241

"Maybe I should thank you."

Well, she didn't come up here just to thank me. I switched off the light so that only the bedside lamp remained on.

I looked at her and she at me. I stepped forward; she backed off.

"What's the matter, sweetie?" I asked.

"I've never been with a man. Please be gentle."

Chapter 2

I jerked awake in the middle of the night and reached out for Ellen. She had gone. My heart pounded as I jumped out of bed and pulled open the drawer in which I kept my money. Nothing. I swore aloud as I hurried into my clothes. I had ten dollars in my pocket and that was the only money I had in the world. I checked my watch as I left my room. It said four-fifty.

Downstairs, I said to the desk clerk, "Is the telegram lady here?"

"Which one do you mean?"

"She said her name was Ellen."

He shook his head. "She was just filling in for someone. Is there a problem?"

"No problem." I went back to my room to figure out what I should do next. At about ten I went back down to the lobby and asked the telegram clerk, "Do you know Ellen, the lady who had your job yesterday?"

"No, but I can find out for you," she replied.

"Please do."

She sent a message and got one back. "Sir, she was hired for one day only and that's all we know."

Next I went to see the manager. I ran it all down for him.

He nodded. "Mr. Stone, how may I help you with your problem?"

"I'm not sure you can."

"Neither am I. Do you have enough money to pay your bill?"

"No. That bitch really shook me down."

"Too bad."

"Look, how about letting me stay here a few more days so I can get a job and pay you back?"

He chuckled. "I'm afraid we can't do that here, Mr. Stone. If you want a meal or a place to sleep or an outfit to wear, you can't say, 'Let me have this now and I'll pay for it whenever I can get the money together.' What's worse, I'm afraid we're going to have to keep your suitcase as collateral; you owe us money and you will get your suitcase back when we get our money."

I stood up and said, "You nasty son of a bitch! That's a bad way of treating someone who's in need! You aren't taking my suitcase or anything else of mine. If you try to stop me, I'll tell the whole town about how your whore of a telegram clerk shook me down!"

I stormed out of his office, went back up to my room, packed up all my belongings and left that hotel forever. Out on the street I bought a newspaper and asked the vendor for suggestions on where to stay for the time being. He referred me to a rooming house a few blocks away. I went in, handed over my money and got the key to a room. The place was quite a flophouse compared to the hotel, but at least I had somewhere to stay.

The next day I went looking for employment and found a job delivering groceries and meat for a big downtown store. Each night I came home feeling beat to shit, but I felt grateful that I had a job and a bed. I reminded myself to be humble and modest.

Chapter 3

My workday began at seven in the morning. Job one was to deliver the early orders. The clerks had them ready the night before, so I would take them out, load them onto the pushcart and deliver them. I didn't much like the work—it was a no-brainer job and I had more brains than any ten people I had ever met—but it paid half-decently and I hoped to save enough money to find out where my uncle and aunt had gone and rejoin them.

But a couple of days later it all came crashing down on me. I had just started packing some items down the street when I suddenly felt ill. Maybe I had been eating too much shitty food; the sidewalk started to make rolling motions and I could scarcely keep my balance. I dropped the order through sweaty, trembling hands and watched in helpless disgust as the eggs and milk turned into a sauce upon the pavement. I wiped sweat from my face and took deep breaths, admonishing myself not to fall.

My boss came out, looked at me, then at the mess I'd made and back at me as I leaned against the building. Sweat poured down my face from my brow to my chin and onto my neck and chest. He made no move to help me and I tried to speak but my words came out as gibberish.

"Come in and get your final paycheck once you've sobered up enough to walk," he told me. Then he went back into the building.

I again tried to speak but nothing came out. He thought I was drunk! As I leaned against the building and did my best to stay conscious, I nearly wept. But I didn't have time to cry or curse; I needed to get my shit together and overcome my dizziness.

By and by it passed. I started feeling mostly human again. I watched as a clerk rushed outside to clean up my mess. I went inside and headed for the glass booth my boss called his office.

"Mr. Duncan—"

"Yes?"

"I'm not drunk, just ill."

"If you're ill, you shouldn't be working. Go

away."

I did as told. I went back to my hotel and didn't look for another job that day. I didn't look for a job, or do much else, for the next several days.

At some point I went outside again and started looking for a job. I could find none and my money soon ran low. I ate only one meal per day and resolved to get out of Dodge. My rent would be due soon and I didn't have the money.

I walked down the street and decided to go back to Vancouver, a place where I had many friends and that I knew well.

I sold my shit at a pawnshop and, with very few personal possessions, I went down to the freight yards. I was going home—back to Vancouver, British Columbia, Canada.

Chapter 4

It wasn't a terribly difficult trip; there were many others like me, some folks on their way to nowhere in particular, while others had specific destinations and objectives in mind.

They were like people all over are—some were kind and polite, but others were less so. I didn't hassle them and they didn't fuck with me.

Eventually I reached Vancouver and I walked around downtown, gawking at all the big buildings like every other dumb tourist.

Suddenly I felt famished. I went into a cafeteria and ate a substantial lunch. When I paid my check I realized that I had only about fifty cents left. But I didn't fret over that. I spent that night in a Downtown East Side flophouse that cost me only a nickel. I fell asleep smiling, knowing that this was my city and I would get by just fine.

It rained as I slept and rained even harder as I awoke. That night I slept in a hallway and had a better night than I expected. When I went outside, the rain had stopped.

I found day work doing general cleanup. Our boss was a fat guy with a big Italian nose.

My job was to rake all the leaves from a nearby park and put those leaves into a big garbage bag.

Presently the boss said to me, "Why you work so slow, kid? You feeling lazy today?"

I showed him my hands and said, "They're red and raw. I'm doing the best I can."

"Your best not good enough," he said.

An hour later one of the other guys said to me, "We knock off for lunch soon."

When lunchtime happened, I ate nothing because I had nothing to eat. One guy said, "I have more than I need. Drink this soup."

I accepted the soup and chugged it down. Right away I felt better.

"Have you been in Vancouver long?" asked the guy who'd given me the soup. He said his name was

Tim.

I shook my head. "Just got in."

"Bloody cold out today," he said.

"Been very wet, too," I replied.

"Where are you staying?"

"Don't have a place yet," I told him.

"Why don't you come stay at my place for a few nights till you get your shit together and figure out where you want to love?"

"Maybe you don't have enough room for me."

"Maybe I do."

Finally the day was over. We followed the foreman back into the office and turned in whatever equipment we had used. Then Tim and I went to his home in the Downtown Eastside. He said to his mother, "Mum, this is Francis Stone. He's homeless for the moment. He's going to stay with us tonight."

I ended up staying there for over a month.

She said, "Francis, you look hungry. We're going to eat now."

We sat down for dinner. She said to her son, "Tim, you better get a nap because you're going to go back to work in a few hours."

He nodded and said to me, "I have two jobs, so I get two paychecks. You want to work with me tonight?"

I nodded.

We took a nap in his bedroom. I was so tired that I fell into a deep sleep. It seemed life fifteen minutes later that he was shaking me awake, saying, "Wake up, Francis! We need to go back to work!"

I nodded and sat up, stupefied by exhaustion. I followed Tim down the street, both of us carrying bag lunches prepared for us by his mother. We worked till six o'clock the next morning, doing routine maintenance. When our shift ended, Tim and I went back to his place, collapsed into bed for three hours, then got up and went back to work again.

Chapter 5

Soon we got laid off. The paymaster handed me twenty dollars, and I felt as if I owned Vancouver. I had looked for work, found some and made money. For the first time in a while I considered myself part of a community.

When I reached Tim's place I offered his mother half of what I had earned. She said, "Keep it—you'll need it."

Tim and I flopped into bed and had a long sleep we desperately needed. When we woke up, his sister said, "Are you two laid off?"

"Yes we are!" he cried out, beaming.

"What will you do now?" she asked me.

"I don't know. Maybe I'll get another job."

"I doubt it. No one's hiring anyone right now."

"I found this one, so I'll find another."

"No you won't," she said.

"Where's Mum?" Tim asked.

"She went to the meeting. She wants you to go there, too."

Tim got up. "Then that's what I'll do now."

They went to that meeting while I stayed at home and waited for them to return. When they did come back, the sister said, "Are you still up? Why aren't you asleep?"

"Not sleepy," I said.

"They're going to be at that meeting for another hour or more. I got so sick of listening to them so I came home."

I sat by the window and looked out at the city. This was the same city I had known altogether my life but each time I looked at it I saw something different.

"Well, goodnight," she said.

"Goodnight to you, too," I replied.

"Aren't you going to sleep?"

"No, I think I'll wait till Tim gets back."

"Could be some time before that happens."

"I'll wait up anyway."

"Well, in that case, would you bring me a glass of water?" she asked from her bedroom.

I did just that, and as I handed her the glass she

drank it down. Then she handed it back to me and caressed my hand. "Want some company?"

"No," I said.

"Afraid?"

"Yes. A little."

"Nobody would have to know."

"*I* would know."

Not long after the meeting, at just after midnight, they came home. The girl was asleep by then. Tim said to me, "It's going to rain hard some more."

I said, "Vancouver is all about rain."

He nodded.

Early the next morning I went out looking for a job but got no offers, just a come-on from the whores on East Hastings Street. I started to think there was a single job to be had in the whole city. Even the nine- and ten-dollar-per-week jobs were unavailable. At some point I went back to Tim's place and told them of my poor luck.

"You'll get something," he said. "Something will turn up."

Chapter 6

At the end of the week I still had no job and very little money.

On Saturday night, Tim asked me, "Do you want to go to a party?"

"Yeah, sure. But maybe—"

"No maybes. We're going to a party tonight."

"It's called a rent party. It costs a quarter. You pay your money, and you get to eat and drink and dance. Lots of ladies there, too."

At the party they served everyone a tumbler of beer with two shots of gin dumped in. I think I was drunk after the first sip. About thirty people were at that party; one guy played a guitar while the people danced.

By three in the morning the party ended. Tim was so drunk he could scarcely move. I half-carried him back to his apartment; the cool Vancouver air cleared my head as I walked down the street. Tim sang and giggled for most of the way, but lost consciousness once we reached his home.

In the hallway, we saw a man hurrying towards us. Tim's sister was shouting, "I want the rest of my money!" The man looked me up and down, frowned at me, so he reached into his pocket, pulled out a few dollar bills and flung them at her. Then he practically ran away from us.

The sister and I put Tim to bed. She said, "You won't tell anyone about what I did earlier?"

I shook my head. "I have no idea what you're talking about."

She said, "We need more money. What we have coming in isn't enough. Welfare doesn't pay us enough, and no boss is paying adequate wages."

"Don't worry," I said. "It will work out all right."

We went to church together in a little store. I felt strange about that; to me, a church should be a big, ornate place where they did rites and rituals and whatnot—if you were going to praise and glorify God, you were supposed to do so in a fancy place.

Tim's mother must have sensed what I was thinking, because she offered me a kind little smile and said, "God is everywhere; and he hears prayers even when they happen in humble places like this."

The others parishioners looked at me with some skepticism because they had never seen me there, but once they saw who I was with they mostly ignored me until the service was concluded and they introduced us around. I liked it when they had me meet the pastor and told him I was their friend.

We went home and sat around, doing very little. I had the nicest time, just hanging out and being lazy.

On Tuesday, Tim and I got some work delivering things. We made three dollars apiece but were unemployed again after that.

Thursday night was when they had their weekly meeting. I sat at home and waited while they did their thing.

Nelly came home early but we didn't say much to each other. We had too many things to think about and too few things to talk about so we just sat there and thought. When the others came home we all went to bed.

The days went by very fast. Soon March arrived and the weather became milder. I grew restless and started to think of living. One day, when Nelly and I were at home alone, I said, "I think I should go soon."

She looked up at me, frowning.

"You didn't think I was going to stay here forever, did you?"

That night at dinner I told the bunch of them that I was leaving. They asked me to stay. "I need to get a job somewhere. I'm leaving tomorrow."

Tim's mum smiled. "Be a good boy, Francis. Remember where we live in case you need us."

Chapter 7

I walked down Granville Street and applied for a job at every store I could find. Some employers were polite about rejecting me; others were not. It all depended upon their mood. On Davie Street I got some work in a cafeteria, washing dishes for the afternoon. Once my shift was over, the manager paid me a dollar and invited me to have lunch there. I stuffed the money into my pocket and ate a large meal. Then I asked him if he needed anyone for the following day.

The man shrugged. "No, I don't. In fact, I didn't even need you today, but you looked so desperate for work—"

I nodded. "O.K., fair enough."

Outside, the sky was getting darker by the moment. I told myself that I had better find myself a flop or I would end up sleeping in Stanley Park. I procured a puny room at a seedy SRO hotel for fifty cents. In the lobby they had a few newspapers; I sat reading them before going upstairs to retire for the night. I wondered what I should do about looking up my aunt and uncle. I sure didn't want them to find me looking this way, indigent and slovenly and unable to care for myself. I also feared encountering someone who knew me; what would I say about my dreadful appearance and lack of visible means of support?

I was up and dressed at seven in the morning downtown. The day-employment agencies as usual were crowded and had nothing for me. They sent me here and there but the bosses had already filled the positions or had someone else in mind. I ate in a cheap restaurant and had franks and beans and coffee for a quarter. I returned to the hotel and rented a bed in a semiprivate room. I had ten roommates that night, mostly men who had not yet hit bottom.. They played cards and made small talk. I eavesdropped on them for a while before I went to sleep.

The next day I went into a warehouse and got a job immediately. The manager said, "What do you want?"

"A job," I replied.

"Not hiring," he said.

Just then his telephone rang and he learned that one of his employees had just quit.

"Why are you still here?" he asked me after hanging up.

"I want a job."

"I said we're not hiring."

"I'm not leaving till you hire me."

He paused. "Got any experience?"

"I have plenty of work experience," I told him.

"How old are you?"

"Twenty."

"You don't want this job. I need a delivery boy. I pay eight dollars per week."

"I want it."

"Why?"

"Because 'm living at a flop right now and I'm pretty desperate. I need money. Whatever job you got, I'll do."

He sighed. "O.K., you're hired. You can start right now if you want."

We shook hands and I thanked him. I told myself that things might actually start improving.

Chapter 8

"The first thing you do is sweep up the store," the manager told me.

I nodded and did as told. The manager whistled and said, "You sweep like you've been doing it all your life."

I smiled. "I've had some experience."

I unpacked boxes and stocked the shelves. I learned quickly enough that I was both sales clerk and delivery boy. I spent the morning keeping busy at my job. The manager came up to me and said, "Let's go. We close for lunch."

We went to a nearby ice cream parlor and had a sandwich and pop. I told him some lies and he told me some, too. Then we went back to work.

"I'm glad you're a fast learner," he said. "I need someone who can learn fast and work hard."

"I'll do the best I can," I told him. "I really need this job."

At seven o'clock we closed up the shop and left.

I walked back to the hotel and took a private room again. I ate at a local restaurant, went for a walk and went back to the hotel. I felt tired and slept well the whole night.

Chapter 9

On Sunday morning I slept late. I checked my bedside clock and saw the time: just about eleven. I smoked a cigarette, in no hurry, to get busy, and thought of the day before.

The past few weeks seemed so long ago. I had never worked in freezing weather nor experienced hunger. I felt good.

I thought about the night before, when Charlie, my boss, told me that the little old guy who'd just come in was *our* boss, the one who owned many stores like the one we worked in. their visit was brief and the two men nodded and smiled. Later on, I bought a bagful of groceries and put it on my tab.

"Who's getting this stuff?" Charlie asked.

"Just some people who were kind to me when I needed some kindness," I said.

I smiled as I finally got out of bed and went down the hallway to take a shower. Then I went over to see Tim and his family.

He opened the door and smiled when he saw me. "Francis! How's it goin', eh? Come on in!"

I stepped inside and he called into the room, "Mum! You'll never guess who's here!" He grabbed my hand and shook it till I thought he would break it. Finally I retrieved it and said, "Nice to see you too."

Soon their mother came in and greeted me. I put the bag of groceries on the table and said, "I got a real job at a grocery store, so I brought you a little something." She sat down and wept.

"Mum," I murmured, putting an arm around her, "what's the matter?"

She looked up at me with a sad little smile. "Nothing, Francis. It's just that I've been praying for you all the time to get something going in your life so that would smile again."

I swallowed hard and looked at the others—Tim, Angus and Nelly—for some clue as to how to react to Mum's words.

Tim nodded. "It's true—Mum said for all of us to pray for you every night, and that's just what we did."

"I don't know what o say," I told them.

Mum shook her head. "You don't have to say anything. All *I* can say is, 'We asked the Lord to give us what we wanted and He said yes and all we can do now is thank Him for His kindness.'"

After eating, Mum said, "This has been a good week for us, too."

"Really?" I asked. "What happened?"

"Nelly got a job too! She's working at a factory and it pays decent money!"

"Nice!" I said, looking over at Nelly, who just stared at me.

"It's hard work and long hours," Mum went on, "but Nelly doesn't mind. She knows she has to keep it up because we're all counting on her."

Soon the others left, leaving just me and Nelly. "So you got a job, eh?"

"Yeah, lucky me."

"What do you do at that factory?"

"Not a factory. Some other kind of place."

"Oh." I knew she meant a brothel. "How did you

end up with that?"

She shrugged. "Easiest job in the world to find. World's oldest profession."

"Can't you find something else?"

"Probably. But why try? Easiest money I'll ever make."

The others came back and had dinner. I left before they ate, because they didn't have enough to go around and I hated the idea of eating their food. I took a walk through Stanley Park and saw a movie at a Granville Street cinema. I can't remember its name, so I guess it wasn't that good.

Chapter 10

By the end of next week life had settled down to a boring routine for me. After work I went to the desk clerk and asked him if he had a vacant room with an adjoining bathroom I could move into indefinitely. He said yes and I got a better room.

Saturday was difficult. I worked long and hard as I looked after customers. I joked with those who wanted to laugh and showed respect to those who demanded to be taken seriously. I worked like hell but enjoyed it.

Sunday with Tim and his family was a somber affair. "Where is everyone?" I asked him.

"Gone out for a walk."

"How are you fixed for work?"

"Something here and there, but not enough."

"Hard luck," I said.

"Tell me about it."

I handed him a dollar. He accepted it with a little nod and stuffed it into his pocket.

"Buy yourself some smokes," I said. "Go see a movie or something fun and stop worrying about everything."

"What, me worry?" he said, doing his best to smile.

Later on, I saw Nelly writhing in agony.

"What's wrong?" I asked her.

"I'm sick."

"Go see a doctor."

"I did. I got the clap."

"From the brothel," I said.

"Yeah. I'm workin' there tonight."

"You'll give it to someone else," I said.

"Too bad for them."

Just then Mum walked in. Nelly rushed up to her and said, "Mum, Francis got Tim a job today!"

"That right, eh?" Mum replied, looking at me.

"Yes," I said. When Tim came in I asked him to go to the store and buy a package of Player's Lights and a big bottle of pop. I think we could all use a cold drink right now."

Tim and Nelly went to the store. Mum said, "Francis, you've been quite a friend to us. Thank you for your kindness."

I blushed. "You've been kinder to me than I've been to you."

After a few moments of silence, she said, "Francis, you seem like a tall, handsome, intelligent young man. Are we the only friends you have? You were born and raised here in Vancouver. Don't you stay in touch with any of the people you've met over the years?"

I immediately thought of Amnon and Clark. "No. The friends I've had have gone their own ways. If I looked them up now, they would probably say, 'Why are you contacting me now?'"

"Real friends are still your friends even if you don't see them for a few years or many years. A person should have as many friends as they can get. You should have friends your own age you can go out with."

"I like you people just fine."

She shook her head. "We're not enough. You need people you have more in common with."

"I like you people just fine," I repeated.

Mum smiled. "I think Nelly likes you just fine, too."

I felt pretty sure that Mum knew little or nothing about Nelly's employment.

Presently the others came back with the pop and we each had a glass. I watched Nelly drink hers and felt terribly sorry for her because her options in life had been so limited that she had to work in a brothel.

Chapter 11

We sweated like pigs that afternoon in the park. The sun beat down on us without mercy. We bought hot dogs and pop from a vendor and enjoyed those refreshments as we watched the game.

When we got back to the house the time was nearly six o'clock and Tim hadn't come back yet. Nelly was home and she tried to persuade me to stay for dinner but I said no thanks and went to Granville Street to eat. Then I went to see a picture show in the West End and left the cinema a few minutes after ten. I walked over to Tim's place to see if he had come back. I turned up the street and headed out to their place.

On my way I saw a fire engine race past me. I stared after it like a fool till I saw smoke pouring out of a building down the street and realized the fire's location was Tim's home. Then I just ran like hell towards the blaze.

A few dozen people stood there as the firefighters pumped water onto the fire. The cops gave the people a shove backwards and I bulled my way to the front. Then I felt a hand clamping down on my arm. I turned around.

"Tim! I'm glad you're O.K.!"

He frowned. "Where are the others?"

"I don't know. I just got here from the West End."

Then Angus and Nelly ran up to us, shouting, "Where's Mum?"

"I just got here," Tim shouted. "I thought she would be with you."

Angus shook his head. "No, she was feeling tired so she went to bed early."

Tim scowled. "That means she's inside the burning building!"

He hurried towards the building but a couple of cops grabbed him. "Can't go in there," they told him. "It's dangerous."

"But my mum's in there!" he screamed. "I need to

go get her!"

"The firefighters will save her!" one of the cops yelled.

Tim threw a punch at the cops, who blocked it and knocked Tim cold. The cop lay him down on the ground and said to the people, "I didn't want to do that but he couldn't go in. The building is going up in flames."

Someone in the crowd shrieked. I saw Nelly dash into the inferno as Angus sat crying over his unconscious brother. I chased Nelly into the building.

"Nelly! Don't do it! Come back!" I yelled.

Interlude

YAEL

It is peculiar, Amnon was thinking, *that no matter how hard Clark tried, he failed to understand Francis. Really, none of us thought of Francis in quite the same way. He seemed like a very different person to each of us. I often wondered who the real Francis Stone was. Perhaps the real one didn't exist. Maybe Yael was the only one who really knew him—*

"Want a cocktail?" Clark was asking. Amnon sat back and watched as Clark mixed the highballs. As he turned his head he noticed that Tina was looking at him. He looked back; she smiled; he smiled. Old friends were priceless, the best kind; trouble was, no matter how long you knew them, you never really *knew* them.

He accepted the cocktail from Clark and sipped it,

enjoying the relaxing warmth of alcohol.

Tina said, "I wonder what Yael thought of him."

He nodded. "Was just thinking that. She was the first of us to see the real person behind Francis Stone. The first time she met him—when I brought him home, she checked him out and figured out what he was about—and she didn't like him. She was afraid of him, like she could see right away that he was a gangster in training. She said, 'He's not like a boy at all. He's cold and hard and mean, like he's seen and experienced too much bad stuff already.'" He laughed. "Poor Yael! Back then, he affected her more than he did us, and she was several years older than we were and much more adult. Francis freaked her out a lot.

"That summer, we had a girl living with and working for us. Anya? Was that her name? I think it was. But who cares? She was about twenty, a very pretty girl in every way. Anyway, Francis surely looked at her and thought, 'I want *that* one.'

"That evening, Francis had given me a black eye because of a boxing lesson and Yael was pissed off at him about it. She bitched at him about it but regretted her bitching the moment he left. She said, 'Maybe I was too hard on him. He's an orphan who has never had any friends.'

"Later on, Yael wanted to speak privately to Anya because she had some things on her mind. As she approached Anya's door, she could hear a man's voice. Yael hustled back to our apartment and went to the part where she could see into Anya's kitchen. That was where she saw Anya and Francis making out. There was nothing innocent about it; those two were going at it like sexually experienced adults.

"Yael realized soon enough that Anya had gotten what Yael most wanted—a lover, preferably Francis. *Preferably* Francis? No, *definitely* Francis. She was a woman who was ready to be with a man, and that man was already being intimate with someone else.

"Years later, she started working at the welfare unit of Vancouver Centennial Hospital. You remember that, right, Steve? Your father had called in a few favors and helped her get that job. I was an intern at Simon Fraser Hospital and got in at around three in the morning. The light was on so I went in find out why Yael was still up at that ludicrous hour. I found het sitting in the recliner, staring straight ahead.

"She said, 'I just saw Francis.'

"I said, 'Francis who?'

"She said, 'You know, *Francis*.' Then she said, 'Amnon, you wouldn't know him today. He's underweight and his hair is white. He looks awful. They brought him in for mental illness and malnutrition. He passed out on the street. The doctor said the poor bastard hadn't eaten in days.'

"I shook my head and said, 'I'm missing something here. Who are we talking about?'

"She rolled her eyes and said, 'Francis. Francis Stone.'

"Suddenly I was as surprised as she was. 'Francis!' I shouted. 'Where did you see him?'

She said, 'At Vancouver Centennial! That's what I've been trying to tell you!"

"Why was Francis Stone in the hospital?" I asked. "Was he visiting someone?"

"No, he was a patient."

"I've often wondered what became of him," said Steve.

"Maybe I can fill you in," said Amnon.

PART FIVE

Chapter 1

Mac dropped out of school and went to work on the truck. He made decent money and moved in with some friends. By summertime I had learned my job thoroughly and the days went by quite quickly. On Sunday, my one day off, I just mostly hung out and took it easy.

I didn't make friends with everyone the way I used to, but supposed that making friends didn't have to be my top priority in life, either. I did my job, kept my mouth shut and wondered about my aunt, uncle and two cousins. My boss told me he wanted to give me a raise in the next few months, which I took to mean that I could keep my job for as long as I wanted it. I wasn't making the kind of money I had pulled in when I worked for Stelfox, but I wasn't homeless, either, so I did my best to be grateful and humble. One of the reasons my job with Stelfox paid so well as that it was illegal, and illicit work always paid well simply because there was so much danger involved.

Pete, the guy who managed the ice cream parlor where I had eaten so many lunches, asked me if I wanted to work at his place on Sundays, my day off, which was his busiest day of the week. I said yes, and genuinely enjoyed making sundaes and shakes and visiting with the young people who frequented that place. Many of them often went to the club upstairs from the ice cream parlor. They were kind of hush-hush about it, so I decided to check it out for myself, especially because I would be cleaning up downstairs and could hear loud voices coming from upstairs and I needed to know what all that passion was about.

Some of the people from upstairs had invited me to join them but I declined. But on one Saturday night I checked it out. The room was huge and a band played while people danced. Others stood around eating cold cuts and bread and drinking beer.

A guy I knew vaguely came up and shook my hand. "My name's Ross—remember me?"

"A little bit."

"Didn't expect to see you here."

I shrugged. "I wanted to come up here and see

what your game was."

"Well, I'm glad you did." He introduced me to some people and took off. I saw a girl I had encountered in the ice cream parlor and went up to her. She said, "What the hell are you doing here?"

"I'm a member of the party."

She laughed. "Like hell!"

"O.K., I came up for the free food and beer."

"I believe you."

I asked her to dance and she said yes. After a while we sat and Ross went to the microphone. He introduced a man named Gil Cross.

Ross got down, and Gil got up. Everyone cheered at Gil, a young, tall, handsome black man. Presently he held up a hand and everyone went silent.

"Friends," he said, "I look out at you and see some new faces—many new faces—but they're human faces and friendly faces and they're people like us, so I want to thank them for being here tonight and wanting the same things out of life that we want." He sounded vaguely American—how many black people were there in Canada?—but I couldn't place his accent with any precision.

"Tonight I'm not going to talk about the party or its principles, because you already know about those things so well. Instead I'm going to tell you the story of a man who lives down the block.

"He has never been here; he has never attended our meetings. I have asked him here, and so have many others, but he declines our invitation. He was employed, then got laid off and went on welfare till he could find another job. He is afraid that if his bosses find out that he believes in us, they will fire him. This man was recently involved in an industrial accident that was his employer's fault. He is in a local hospital and the doctors do not know if he will survive. We are going to sue his employer over this matter."

Everyone cheered.

"That man's wife is here with us tonight. The money will she receive from the compensation board will not allow her to buy food for her children, much less pay her other living expenses. I know that most of you can scarcely afford to help her out with a few pennies from your own pockets, but I want you to do just that.

"The party will assume the legal expenses associated with this action. But I want you to be big enough to do with a little less and help these people who are in need. You need to remember that what has happened to him can happen to you, too."

I shrugged and took out a dollar bill. I handed it to him.

"That's very generous of you," he said.

"I have a job. I can afford it."

The girl I had danced with came over to me and said, "You were speaking to Gil Cross." She said it as if I had just spoken to God.

"My name is Theresa, by the way. I know that you're Francis from downstairs. So, do you want to take off or hang out here all night?"

"Let's go. But first I have to go to the washroom."

As she walked away, I told myself, *I wouldn't kick her out of bed.*

Chapter 2

I made a date with Theresa for the following afternoon. We were going swimming at English Bay. She was one cute chick but I knew I couldn't get into her pants. She was a born tease; she would talk dirty and make eyes at me, and she would even make out till my tongue went numb; but once I tried to feel her up, she would say no way.

"I don't know about you guys," she said, giggling. "You have sex on the brain. You seem to think that if you take a girl out and show her a good time, you're entitled to some hanky-panky. Why can't you just take her out for dinner and dancing and say goodnight?"

"Because we're guys," I retorted, "and we're horny bastards day and night."

Nothing much happened between us, but because of her I became one of the regulars upstairs. I began to realize that I wasn't the only person in the world who had to break his ass to earn the chump change I needed to buy food and thus survive. So many others had the same problem—no matter who or what they were, they had to make do on piss-poor salaries. Humiliation and degradation put queer little smiles on their faces. Time and hardship had ground them down. Such grinding down manifested itself in different ways.

Some poor folks would come into the store with their food vouchers and make jokes about it—"Wow! We get to eat again!"—as they went along procuring food items till their vouchers were used up. Some would come up to the counter, slap down their vouchers in front of me and say, "Do you take these?" Still others would loiter in the store until everyone else had left and then ask, quietly and with considerable embarrassment, "Do you accept these?"

Upstairs in the club, people found vouchers degrading and demeaning. They wanted poor people to get cash instead of vouchers.

I dated Theresa every Sunday. I didn't want to see her on the weekends because she got me too horny and I felt frustrated, which made me toss and turn all night. I masturbated like a fiend, which only made me feel that much more exasperated.

On Thursday afternoon I made a delivery to someone's house. I rang the bell and the door opened. A young woman stood before me; she had faded blonde hair and wore an old dress. A new customer, she had used up her food voucher and had bought some items to be delivered later on that dau, when she expected to have some cash to pay for her purchases.

"Groceries," I said. "A dollar twenty-five, please." My boss, Charlie, had always admonished me to get the cash before I left the customer's doorway.

"Bring it in, please," she said to me, "and put it in the kitchen."

I did so, and she said, "My husband will be home soon with cash. Why don't you leave it here and I'll come by with the money later?"

I shook my head. "My boss would go bananas if I failed to collect on a delivery."

"Then just wait a few moments till he gets in." A child entered the room, a girl scarcely of school age, and the young picked her up. "Sit down if you like," she said to me.

I nodded and sat at the kitchen table. I lit a cigarette and offered her one; she declined. I smoked till my cigarette was little more than a stub. "Look, ma'am, I really have to get going. My boss will wonder where I've gone to."

"Please just wait a few more minutes. I'm sure he'll be along."

"Can't do it. Tell him to come to the store with money and we'll give him the stuff when he pays us."

"But we're hungry and we need to eat. My husband went to find a job."

"Ma'am, I'm just the messenger. I have no say-so in this matter. If you have any questions, ask my boss."

She was a young woman and I was a young man. She looked at me and I at her. We were both thinking the same thing: She had something I wanted and vice versa. Ordinarily she wouldn't spread her legs for anyone except her husband...but these were not ordinary times.

She sent her child out of the room. We went into

her bedroom. She started unbuttoning her dress and wiped a tear that slid down her cheek.

"You can just keep the groceries," I told her.

"But I thought you wanted—"

"I don't want it that badly."

I left their home and walked down the street. Soon I saw the girl, who was now with her father.

"Guess what!" she shouted at me. "My daddy got a job!"

"Congratulations!" I shouted back.

Chapter 3

The next morning the lady who had offered herself to me came to the store with her daughter. She squared her shoulders as she walked up to me and made eye contact. I liked her self-assurance.

"My husband got a job," she said. "I wonder if you would let me pick up a few things on credit, till he gets paid."

I nodded. "I'll ask my boss." He told me to make the decision myself, so I told her to pick out whatever she wanted. As I did so I apologized for our encounter the day before. She said nothing; she just gathered up her purchase and left the store.

Later on, Theresa came in. "Coming to the meeting tomorrow?" she asked.

"I'll be there."

After she left, my boss said, "Why do you go to

those meetings, anyway? Want to know who goes to those things? A bunch of bums, that's who."

"They're making the best of a bad situation. Besides, I don't have many friends and at those meetings they seem to like me."

"I just hope you're not going to become a Communist."

I frowned. "What's a Communist?"

The months went by. Mack quit his job and went to live with some relatives. Gil Cross came by and I said, "I'm just on my way to dinner."

"Mind if I join you?" he asked.

"Please do. I always like to have someone to talk to while I'm eating."

"Have you been in Vancouver all your life?"

"Born and raised…but I've spent time in a few other places."

"How old are you?"

"Twenty-two." Then, "Hey, I suppose I don't mind these questions, but why are you taking this sudden interest in me?"

"I'm interested in you because I am. You're an interesting person."

I laughed. "Am I? I think I'm very much like all the others."

"Do you really think so?"

"Yes."

We went into a cafeteria and ate.

"You have gray in your hair," Gil told me. "You seem much older than you are. You just hang back, checking it all out, not saying much."

"I guess."

We talked some more and went our separate ways. I genuinely liked him and looked forward to seeing him again.

Chapter 4

The winter of 1932-33 was dreadful. So many people were unemployed and on welfare. Even I, who had a half-decent gig as a full-time employee who collected steady paychecks, that the government needed to intervene with public policy that insured adequate employment for everyone. People were cold, hungry and desperate. They could kid themselves about being able to see prosperity coming soon, but I knew that was just so much bullshit.

But I needed to be honest with myself. The hard times were all around but they didn't affect me. The old joke went that a recession was when your neighbor lost his job; a depression happened when you lost yours. Well, no bad economic shit had happened to me just yet, so I had no reason to bitch.

Whenever I went upstairs to attend those meetings the myriad complaints I heard seem to enter one of my ears and exit the other. The rest of the audience listened and nodded with much empathy but nobody seemed to have the slightest idea of how to generate jobs and end poverty.

Men who went out every morning looking for work now slept late and said, "What the fuck? Why look for a job when no one's hiring?" At one point every other store on East Hastings Street seemed to close, and nobody gave a good goddamn.

Everyone one seemed confused, even bewildered. They wanted—needed?—to blame someone but didn't know who.

The bad winter went on into February. On one bitterly cold evening in that month, I saw Gil Cross cry.

I stood in the very back of the room. The place was half empty and those who were there stood in small groups speaking to each other in hushed voices. No band played; no one danced—that money went towards more important things. Many people had ceased attending the meetings altogether. They had given in to despair.

Gil had climbed onto one of the tables to address the room. "Beautiful people—"

Just then a rock smashed through the window, then another and a third and fourth. Gil just stood there on the table, his mouth hanging open.

I stood nearest the window, so I looked out and saw twenty or more men down below shaking their fists at me. I felt someone grab my hand. I looked over and saw Theresa.

"Who are they?" she asked, her voice unsteady. "What do they want?"

"Damned if I know," I muttered.

Then someone from the street shouted, "Get that bastard down here! He screwed my wife! He screwed everyone's wife!"

I looked over at Gil. He swallowed hard and looked away.

"Someone should call the cops," a woman said.

Gil shook his head. "No, I'll go talk to them." He started for the door.

"Don't let him go, Francis," Theresa said. "They want to kill him."

"Gil," I said, "don't go out there just yet. Let's make the crowd allow the women to leave, then we'll deal with those guys and find out what they want." I looked out the window and shouted, "If we send him down there, will you let the women go home?"

They muttered to each other for several moments. Then one of them said, "O.K., we'll do it."

"The women will come out," I called out, "then the men. Finally it will be just Gil and me. Fair enough?"

"O.K.," said the man.

Theresa whispered, "Francis, you're crazy. They'll kill both of you."

"No," I said. "When you get home, call the cops. They'll come out here and help us."

One of the men said, "The crowd wants to kill Gil, and the cops won't care. They think he's a troublemaker."

Someone from the street yelled, "Bring that bastard to the window so we can see that he's really there."

I called Ross over and instructed him to up to the roof and open the trap so we could get right out. Then he needed to rejoin us so we could leave the building together. He nodded and left.

"The rest of you," I said, "leave the building now.

Walk nice and slow."

They did as told. They made no sound as they exited the building. I watched from the window as the first of them left the building, walked past the crowd and disappeared.

Someone in the crowd yelled, "So where **is** that bastard?"

I made a come-over-here gesture to Gil and he joined me at the window. He looked out, his handsome face expressionless, lips a straight line. I peered past the crowd and saw Theresa as she and some other women walked to the corner. She turned around, offered me a half-wave and disappeared with the other women. Another rock came sailing up towards us. It whizzed by me but struck Gil on the cheek. He did not flinch. The rock ripped open his skin and blood streamed down his face.

"Do you know them?" I asked him.

He nodded.

I guessed that many of them had been members here at one time or another, which was how they— and their wives—had come to know Gil.

Just then I heard Ross whisper, "Francis!" I

whispered "O.K.?" and he whispered, "Yeah!"

I yelled to the crowd, "We're coming down!" and followed Ross to the top floor. I could hear the men downstairs swearing, and then they entered the building. Ross, Gil and I entered the roof just as the men got to the top floor.

We went from one rooftop to the next, entered its building and locked the door behind us. Presently we reached East Hastings Street and got into a taxicab.

"You're hurt bad," I told Gil. "Take us to St. Paul's Hospital," I said to the driver.

He did just that, and soon an intern was stitching up Gil's face as I gave the nurse the information she needed. The doctor gave Gil some painkillers and told him to take it easy for a while.

"You better go home now," I said to Gil. "You look like you're about to topple over."

He nodded and smiled. "Thanks, Francis. You were a big help tonight."

"I'll go with you. Where do you live?"

"Maybe I should go to my friend's house tonight," he said.

I shrugged. "It's your call. But we better go there

now. You really look like you need some rest."

We hailed a taxi and I gave the driver an address. We drove off. The drive too several minutes; Gil nodded off and for a moment or two I feared he had died. But then he woke up and I felt better. I tried to tell myself that things would work themselves out and the economy would improve but I didn't quite believe my own words.

Chapter 5

Our taxi stopped in front of a small renovated apartment house that, like a hundred others in Vancouver, had once been a big, imposing single-family house. Gil and I got out. I paid the driver and we entered the building. We went up one fight and found his friend's suite. He winced at the pain from his injured face as he rang the bell.

We waited at the door and he rang the bell some more but nobody answered. "Maybe he's not in," I said, "Shit. We came all this way for nothing."

"I have a key," he said, reaching into his pocket and taking out a sliver of metal. He opened the door and we went in.

"You can go now," he said. "It's late and you must be tired."

"I'll go as soon as I see that you're asleep," I told

him.

He drank a cup of tea and took a couple of pain pills. He changed into blue pajamas and said, "Tell me something, Francis. Back at the club? When all those guys showed up and wanted to kill me? Were you scared?"

"Terrified," I told him.

"You were not. You stared them down, like, 'Fuck you! You don't scare me!'"

I smirked. "The best time to pretend you're fearless is when you're scared shitless."

Soon he crawled into bed and went to sleep. I suddenly felt exhausted and decided to take a nap on one of the chairs. I closed my eyes and nodded off. I woke up to the sound of someone unlocking the door. I glanced up at the clock and saw the time: 2:45 in the morning. The door opened and I watched as a young woman walked in. As soon as she spotted me she stopped and frowned.

"Who are you?" she asked.

She was gorgeous—dark red hair, large brown eyes, full pink lips, even white teeth. Her coat was open and I could see the twin swells of her breasts.

Everyone was the right size and located in the right place. No wonder Gil wanted me to fuck off—I was a handsome man and he didn't want her to meet me. He didn't want the competition.

I stood up so she could see how nice and tall I was. "My name is Francis Stone. I'm a friend of Gil."

"And where is Gil?"

"Asleep in the other room."

She nodded. I could see an ironic little twist to her mouth—I guessed that she felt not altogether displeases to come home to Gil and his handsome young tall friend.

The woman went into the bedroom, looked at Gil and came back out.

"Just a small cut," I said. "He'll live."

"So what happened, anyway?"

I told her and she shook her head.

"Sounds horrible," she said.

I shrugged. "Could have been much worse." Then, "I better go now. I only waited here so that his friend would get home and would be here for him in case he needed some help."

She shook her head. "No, you don't need to go.

I don't know where you live, but you look beat to shit. You can sleep in there with Gil; I'll sack out here on the sofa."

"Not necessary. I'll just go now." I started for the door.

"Wait. You don't understand—I'm his wife." She ran a hand through her hair.

I gave her a sad little smile. "If you're his wife, I'm sorry about his infidelities—but it's none of my business. I'm just grateful that things weren't worse tonight than they could have been, and I'm grateful to be able to say that Gil is a friend of mine."

She eased herself into a chair and let out a huge sigh. "I'm sorry. I lied. I'm not his wife. I wish I was. I wish I could be the woman he needs me to be."

She stared at me and I stared back. I heard my stomach growl. I patted my stomach and said, "This is a hell of a way to treat a guest. Don't you have any food around here to offer me? I'm really famish, Miz—"

"My name is Mary Anne Fahey. I have eggs."

"Anything else, Mary Anne?"

"Nope. I got eggs. Beggars can't be choosers.

314

You want 'em fried or scrambled?"

Ten minutes later we were sitting at her kitchen table. I was devouring her eggs as she talked to me.

"Gil wouldn't have liked it that I told you I was his wife. He says it's always better to be honest and truthful."

I nodded. "Gil is a smart man."

"We met as students at university. You know how it is—one moment you're talking about classwork, then you're talking about other, more personal stuff.

"I was the ballsy one, so to speak. We'll destroy the proletariat and bring about a new world order. What use is today's morality? Who cares what others think? We'll show the bastards that they shouldn't try to grind us down. But Gil didn't say anything. He would just smile. I didn't really know what was going on inside of him.

"I guess he knew that my talk of 'let's save the world from itself' was just my natural youthful enthusiasm. I think he aspired to become a writer or reporter of some consequence and enjoy a middle-class lifestyle but since he didn't seem to have that option, he started studying radical politics."

Just then Gil got up and came to the bedroom doorway. "I see you two have met."

The two of them went to bed and I slept on the sofa in the living room. At one point I saw someone come out and noticed it was her. She came over to me and said, "Why aren't you asleep?"

"Too worried about things to sleep."

"You sound like Gil." She came over and kissed me goodnight. I reached for her breasts. She slapped away my hand. "I'm not yours," she said.

I nodded and rolled over to sleep. I woke up very early, before they did, and sneaked out like a burglar.

Chapter 6

A few minutes after we opened the store, Theresa came in, mad as all hell. "You said you were going to contact me last night!" she practically screamed.

I shrugged. "Couldn't do it. Gil was pretty banged up and I had to stay with him. I spent the night on his sofa."

"I thought those guys were going to kill him because he screwed their wives."

"They didn't get the chance, thanks to me."

"What about the club?"

"What about it?"

She shrugged. "They wanted a new world order or whatever, so I guess that won't happen."

We walked outside and stood on the sidewalk as we looked up at the club, with its broken windows and graffiti. "All over now," she said.

"Maybe not. The people who started the club will get over last night's craziness and start the club all over again." Then, "What did the club mean to you? I mean, what was there for you?"

"It was a social thing. I met people; we ate and drank and laughed and danced. The political talk didn't interest me much."

"The political talk was the whole reason for the club's existence," I told her. I said goodbye and went back to work.

The telephone rang and my boss answered it. "It's for you," he said.

"Hello?"

"Francis, it's Gil."

"Gil! Feeling any better?"

"A little. I'm calling to invite you to dinner."

"Where?"

"At Mary Anne's place."

I said no and we hung up, but it gratified me to know that the invitation was her idea.

Gil called me again the following week and we

had dinner in the West End near Stanley Park. Our conversation was long and fun. I soon figured out why so many seemed to like him so much. He was remarkably smart and quite friendly, the first such charming person I had met in a long time.

"So," I asked over dessert, "what are you going to do now?"

"I'm moving to Seattle, to do the same things I've been doing here."

"I'm not sure what you've accomplished here in Vancouver. These people who joined the club just wanted to have fun. They weren't interested in establishing a new world or saving the human race from itself."

"But over time they would have started getting more interested in those things. That would have happened sooner or later."

"So you're moving to the States," I muttered.

I didn't see Gil again for the rest of the day. I began seeing less of Theresa; the club moved farther down East Hastings Street. Since meeting Mary Anne I had decided that Theresa was cute and sweet but awfully dumb and I wanted to be around intelligent women.

On one spring evening, while we were standing in her hallway, I leaned over and kissed Theresa and she pushed me away. I didn't manhandle her; we just stood there looking at each other.

"You've changed, Francis," she said.

"Have I?"

'Yes. You're not the same. You have some big things on your mind."

"*You're* the big thing on my mind."

'Don't be smart. I have some things on my mind, too. I think we should terminate our relationship, such as it is. I'm getting married. He is a bus driver and makes good money. We can move to Kitsilano and have all the middle-class goodies I've always wanted. Those people at the club are radicals who want to save the world from itself. I'm not them. I just want to live well and be happy."

I sighed and did my very best to hide my big smile. Her news delighted me.

She stuck out her hand. "Let's part as friends, all right?"

I shook my head. "No, you can't mean it."

"Yes, I do." She swallowed hard. I saw tears in her eyes.

"Maybe you're right," I said. "I'm not good enough for you. I wish you well in your new life."

She burst into tears and ran upstairs. I walked out of there and into the street, chuckling.

A month later, as I walked into a restaurant to meet up with Gil, I saw Mary Anne sitting at the table with him. I went over to sit with them.

"Mary Anne will be dining with us," Gil said with a smile.

"Nice for us," I said. "How goes it?" I asked her.

She shrugged. "I'm keeping busy, just like you."

"Nature calls," said Gil. He got up and strode to the washroom.

I pretended to peruse the menu so I wouldn't have to converse with Mary Anne.

"Talk to me, Francis," she said. "Are you surprised to see me here?"

"Kind of."

"I wanted to see what you looked like in the daylight."

"I hope you're not disappointed." I looked out the window. The Vancouver sky had mostly darkened. The city got dark sooner each day. I liked the sunshine. I wished it would come back. I wished that Mary Anne would go away and take the darkness with her.

She smirked and leaned over towards me. "Francis, I think you fear me—you think I'm an evil woman or something."

"I don't think you're anything at all. You just don't interest me. I'm Gil's friend, not yours."

"You've hurt me feelings," she said with a little pout. Then, "Francis, don't you think it's possible for a woman to be in love with two men at the same time? Gil is a wonderful man—kind and sweet and brilliant—but you're quite another—selfish and wicked and dishonest. You're always checking people out and wondering what they can do for you. Therefore, you fascinate me. You don't want to see me but I want to see you, so that's why I got Gil to bring me along."

"And Gil can eat his meal with us knowing very well that I'm going to keep my hands off his woman."

Just then Gil returned and Mary Anne and I pretended we hadn't spoken those words to each other.

After dinner I walked back to my hotel thinking, *If it wasn't for Gil I would bang Mary Anne.* But I put the thought out of my mind and felt ashamed for thinking it.

Chapter 7

I smiled up at the springtime Vancouver sky. Springtime in Vancouver! What a wonderful feeling! Some rainless days to look forward to! Of course, we never really knew how much decent weather spring and summer would bring.

One evening Gil asked if I could get a few hours off because he was going to make a speech in Stanley Park and he wanted me to hear it. I said I would check with my boss.

I hadn't seen Mary Anne in quite some time. I wondered if she would be there and if I still had feelings for her. I supposed I did, and those feelings were part of the reason I wanted to attend Gil's speech, because normally speeches bored me shitless.

Well, I went, and they had erected a stage for speakers. A sign said that Gil was the fourth speaker on the schedule. His speech would be about equality, a subject that he cared about more than just about anything else.

I bulled my way to the front of the crowd. A man stood talking at the microphone. I didn't know who he was or what he was talking about, nor did I especially care. All I wanted was to find Gil. Soon I did—he sat at the back of the stage with some other men, all of whom clearly were waiting to speak. I waved at him.

His head rotated this way and that, as if he were checking out the crowd. He saw me as I waved and he smiled with a small nod. I looked around for Mary Anne. She wasn't there.

I felt a tap on my shoulder and turned around. Theresa smiled at me. "Hey," I said. "Nice to see you. Didn't think you would be here."

"I'm here because Gil is here," she told me.

"Oh." I saw Theresa every day at the store. I kept looking around to see Mary Anne.

"Gotta go. See ya." Theresa took off.

I saw Gil leave the stage and walk towards the washroom. I hurried up to him and said, "How's it goin', eh?"

He beamed and shook my hand. "Glad you

came! I was really nervous about giving this speech till I saw you in the crowd. Then I felt better. This is the biggest crowd I've ever addressed."

"Is Mary Anne here?"

"Naw. Huge crowds freak her out."

He went off to the washroom and then rejoined the others on stage.

I looked around the crowd. The event had an equal-opportunity turnout—poor people, wealthier people, desperate people, smug people. Some of them had probably been born and raised in Vancouver and had shown up to find out why they are impoverished and miserable. Not far away were Vancouver cops on horseback. They gripped batons and eyeballed the masses.

As the next speaker had his say, I felt thirsty so I stepped off to the side and bought a bottle of pop. I drank it as I went back to the crowd, pushed my way forward again and got to the front of the stage. I finished my pop but couldn't figure out where to put the bottle so I just held onto it.

I knew a fight had started when I saw some men wrestling each other in front of the stage. Gil rushed over to break it up and the mounted cops came over and started swinging their batons. Gil somehow ended up underneath one of the horses.

Panicking, I raced out of that scene like so many of the others and soon reached the store. I wished Gil would call me and tell me he was all right. Instead, Theresa called me. "Francis," she said, "you better leave town. The Man is after you. They think you're a shit disturber."

"Where's Gil?"

"Don't you *know*? He's *dead*. The *pigs* got him."

I hurried over to Charlie and said, "I quit."

Chapter 8

So I did the only logical thing—I moved to Atlantic City. I got a job right away because everyone was hiring. I worked at a soda fountain and made half-decent money. My job would end in September. I was fine with that; by then I would probably be sick of that soda fountain. I took a room at a boardinghouse a few blocks away from my new place of employment as I taught myself my job. After clerking at that grocery store in Vancouver I had learned plenty about working in retail and my soda-place gig soon presented no challenge at all.

I spent plenty of time at the beach, then went to work and got lots of sleep. The time went by fast. I didn't bother to make friends with anyone, though many of the people I encountered each day wanted to hang out with me. At the public library I read copies of the Vancouver newspaper but couldn't find any mention of Gil or the cops.

I spent hours thinking of my aunt, uncle and Mary Anne. I missed them all and wondered where they were and what they were doing at each moment.

July passed by very fast and so did August. In a few weeks I would lose my job and return to Vancouver. I looked forward to going home and seeing my old friends.

In late August, as I lay on the beach, I began to think of Mary Anne and, before I could think better of it, I called her.

"Mary Anne?"

"*Francis?*"

"Yes, it's me."

"Where are you?"

"In Atlantic City."

"How are you and when are you coming home?"

"I'm fine and I'll be back soon."

"I want to see you, Francis. I have so many things to say…"

"I have a job here. I can't just run off."

"Then I'll go to you."

"I'm so busy…you'd spend very little time with me."

"Well, that would be better than not seeing you at all."

"It's a six-hour flight, you know."

"I'm already there," she said.

"Mary Anne," I said. "Mary Anne."

"Do you love me, Francis? Do you love me?"

The next day, while at work, I felt a pair of feminine hands over my eyes. "Guess who?" she asked.

"I have no idea," I retorted.

"If you fuck this up, I'm flying right back home."

I took her hands off my eyes and spun her around. "I really didn't think you would fly out here. I thought you were bullshitting."

She smiled. "No bullshit here."

I finished my shift and we walked along the beach I said, "I'll never leave you, Mary Anne."

Chapter 9

Mary Anne and I went swimming. She had a beautiful figure and looked marvelous in her swimsuit. She moved wit feline grace, swaying her hips just so, and I felt very proud to be her man. I noted with satisfaction how the other men licked their lips as they stared at her.

I bought us hot dogs and pop and as we ate and drank, I asked her how she liked Atlantic City. She shrugged and said she supposed it was fun but she felt just as glad to be back home.

"Did you go to Gil's funeral?" I asked her.

She looked at the ground and shook her head.

"Why not?"

"Because I couldn't bear to think of him as dead."

"He was a stand-up guy," I said. "It's a shame he's gone. Only the good die young, as the saying goes."

She eyeballed me. "Do you really mean that, Francis? Maybe, deep down inside, you're glad that things worked out as they did because it brought you and me together, which wouldn't have happened otherwise."

"You're probably right. I can't pretend that there was no upside for me to all of this." To change the subject, I said, "You're looking gorgeous, Mary Anne. But I'm sure you're quite aware of that."

She smirked. "You're looking pretty hot yourself. I'm sure those chicks in Atlantic City were hitting on you all the time."

I laughed. "They kept forgetting I was there."

Chapter 10

Holiday week arrived—those seven busy days between Christmas and New Year's Day. I saw so many people dressed up, smiling, happy to be doing their thing during this festive time. I also saw people looking harried or full of despair, folks who felt that the yuletide season was about friends and family; it could be a difficult season to cope with if you had neither friends nor family around you.

I watched it all from my window and realized that I, too, saw little to be happy about, and I got angry and resentful whenever I saw happy people whose faces were pink with Christmas cheer. I thought of my childhood in the orphanage and hardscrabble life. So many people had better, or at least easier, lives than I did. Damn them!

On New Year's Eve, horns honked and people

staggered about half-drunk. Not me, though, and I wasn't sure why not. I drank and drank, but all it did for me was to make me feel even more morose. I had long since returned to Vancouver Mary Anne, many of her friends and I were at a nightclub in downtown Vancouver. I stood apart from them and inwardly laughed at their foolishness in celebrating the end of one year and the start of the next—were they really rejoicing over the passage of time? Didn't they know that time was our natural enemy, that they were embracing the inevitability of their own deaths? What imbeciles!

Mary Anne approached me. "Having fun, darling?"

I said nothing but pulled her into my arms and kissed her lips. She tasted fine. I started kissing her neck and then her breasts. She wrenched my head from her chest. "Not here," she said, her voice little more than a purr.

I laughed and so did she. We laughed together for the longest time and stared at each other.

By and by midnight came and went. We all went our separate ways. I said goodnight and went outside.

The Vancouver night looked clear and starry but I could see the first hint of dawn far off on the horizon. I resolved not to care about the morning or the day after or the day after that. They could take care of themselves.

Chapter 11

I must have walked a zillion miles before realizing that I still held Gil's picture in my hand. I started to get hungry and felt very tired because I had slept very little, so I went into an all-night cafeteria and had toast and coffee while I turned some ideas up and down in my mind.

By the time I had finished eating I decided to go to a hotel and get some sleep so that I would feel mentally more competent to make life plans. Tomorrow I would begin seeking employment; I was sure that this time I would do all right. I walked along the street in the brisk, clear morning and noticed how empty the streets were; then I remembered that today was the New Year and therefor many people had the day off. I noticed a man hurrying in front of me. I paid relatively little attention to him as he practically groped his way along storefronts. Was he drunk and in need of these buildings for support?

Then he disappeared into a doorway. I shrugged and walked along. A car drove slowly along the street towards me. I made a note of it only because of its very low rate of speed. I heard the rat-tat-tat of gunfire as the car went past the doorway the man had disappeared into. Then the vehicle sped up and turned the corner. At first I froze, clueless as to what, if anything, to do. I headed over to the doorway and the man staggered out. He called, "*Francis*! Help me!"

Aldo Chies. I dropped my bag and gathered him up into my arms. I dumped him off at St. Paul's Hospital and took off. I checked into a hotel but could not sleep. I lay there thinking of Chies and how little he had changed, and how much *I* had. I thought it weird how quickly he recognized me.

I lay in bed and stretched out. I thought of Mary Anne and Gil. When I knew Mary Anne I spent plenty of time at her home and read most of her many books. Some were good, others not. But all of them failed to provide the answers I sought to life's most vexing questions. I wondered why people had always liked me so much when I often gave them v=many reasons to dislike me.

I missed Mary Anne. I slept through the days. I had felt very exhausted. But at night, unable to sleep further, I was overcome by a suffocating loneliness. I longed to pick up the telephone and dial Mary Anne's number, to hear her sweet soft voice.

But no. I could not do that; I could never go back. At last I fell asleep and dreamed of her. Mary Anne, Mary Anne, even in my sleep you seduce me!

I woke up. The sun streamed through my window and hit me in my face. I threw my arm over my eyes but knew that denying the morning and new day would accomplish nothing. With a reluctant grunt I got out of bed, showered, got dressed and left my key with the desk clerk. I would have to move out— two dollars per day was too expensive for me.

I bought a copy of the *Times* and read it want ads, reasonably sure that the job I sought would not be listed therein. I was right; then I headed over to the employment agency and found nothing. I shrugged and chuckled; this day, and hundreds of others to follow just like it, were mine—I did not have to worry, at least not yet.

Two months later I remained unemployed and when I said to myself each morning, *The day is yours. You own it. You can make big things happen today*, I found it more difficult to believe my own optimistic bullshit. Each day seemed a mirage; from a distance, I saw all the goodies I wanted from life sparkling and ready to be snatched up by me; but as soon as I got close enough to reach out and grab a handful, those treasures disappeared. Even the month of March was bitterly cold; I had pawned my most valuable items and had no heavy coat to wear. I hadn't eaten a sensible meal in the longest time and had warded off starvation only by standing in line at soup kitchens. Unable to find day labor, I started to wonder if I would ever get another job.

I traipsed over to Mary Anne's building and rang her buzzer, unsure of what I would say to her when she appeared in the doorway. But some man stood there instead, and when I asked about her, he just said, "Oh, Miss Fahey? She has left town. So sorry."

I walked back down the street and fell down. The longest time passed before I could get back up again.

Chapter 12

They put me into a long gray room that contained about forty beds. The doctor came by in the evening to have a look at me. The nurse accompanied him. He stood at the side of the bed and said, "How do you feel now?"

I shrugged. "Better, I guess."

"You're not eating. What's that all about?"

"Not hungry. The food here is shit."

"We're going to keep you here for observation for a day or two. Is there anything you need right now?"

"I'm craving a cigarette."

"What's your brand?"

"What have you got?"

He tossed me a package of Camels and a book of matches. "Keep the smokes. I've promised myself I'm quitting."

I smiled and thanked him. He and the nurse went away. I smoked and reminded myself just how much better fresh cigarettes tasted than those I had picked up off the street. I also told myself how much better I felt when I had a full meal in my stomach and a clean bed to sleep in.

A female voice to my left asked, "Are you awake?"

"Who wants to know?" I looked over and saw a young woman standing there with forms and a pencil. "I'm here to help you. We have forms to fill out."

"O.K." There was something very familiar about her.

"What is your name? There was nothing in your clothing to give us that information."

"My name is Francis Stone."

"What is your address?"

"I don't have one. I'm homeless. I want you to write that down so that whoever reads it will know that there was a guy in Vancouver named Francis Stone and he was homeless." I looked at her again, sure as all hell that I knew her from somewhere.

Then she smiled, and I knew she was Amnon Lichtmann's sister Yael. I really hoped she didn't recognize me; I didn't want an old friend to see what a wretch I'd become.

She looked at me and I at her. "You're Francis Stone from the orphanage. Your best friend was my brother, Amnon. You must remember us."

"Sorry," I said.

"That was eight years ago. You're ill right now. Maybe you don't remember things."

"Maybe I don't."

"Well, *I* remember plenty. Do you remember a girl named Anya? She lived with us and worked for us. You came over and gave my brother boxing lessons. Remember Clark Rutledge and Tina? Your aunt and uncle? Surely you remember some of them...?"

I shook my head and closed my eyes.

"I've upset you. Remember that there was Anya and later Tina—I was envious of them because everyone liked you. I liked you, too, though I pretended I didn't. You kissed me and said we would always be friends. Remember?"

"Nope."

She leaned forward and said, "Look, I can see that you're tired and I've upset you. I don't want to upset you—I want to help you. Please think hard. We were all the best of friends—you, me, Amnon, Steve, Anya, Tina. Don't you remember any of us?" Then, "Tomorrow I'll bring down two guys—Amnon Lichtmann and Clark Rutledge—who will know you right away, Maybe you'll know them, too."

"Don't bother. I won't know them." I sure as hell didn't want those guys to see me in such awful shape.

"My brother's a doctor at another hospital. He'll come by to see you. We will have many things to say to you."

There were a bunch of things I wanted to ask them about our old gang.

"Whatever, lady," I said with a sigh. "Do what you got to do. But it won't make any difference."

"O.K. Maybe. We'll see tomorrow." She walked away without another word. I lit a cigarette with trembling hands. Tomorrow Amnon and Clark would come by to see me? Bullshit to that! I would have to get out of that mental hospital by then. I would devour a big breakfast tomorrow and skedaddle. They had no legal right to keep me there, anyway.

The following morning I spoke to the doctor and he agreed that I had the right to be discharged if I wanted such a thing. I said I did and he signed the order. I hurried out of there and went into downtown Vancouver in search of Aldo Chies. He owed me one.

Interlude

FRANCIS

Clark walked over to the bar and fixed himself a cocktail. He tasted it and smiled. He turned to Amnon and said, "Sit." Then, "Those lost years. The way you spoke that phrase summed it up just right for me. During that period of time—from when he ran away till the time he turned up next—Francis was growing up too. Not in the sense that you and I were, but in his own way he was maturing. Something must have happened to him during that time to turn him back to the only lifestyle he had ever known that worked well for him.

"I don't know what it was, and I probably will never know. But some significant things happened to him that convinced him that he was destined to spend

349

his life as a criminal.

"It started, weirdly enough, a little while after I had started working as a Crown prosecutor in the 'Thirties. We had a case about a gangland shooting and out of nowhere is this guy who's a real up-and-comer named Francis Stone. I had kind of hoped he wouldn't end up with the Mob."

The boys were sitting at a table playing chump-change poker when the door opened and a man walked in. The others took a moment to look at him. He was tall and thin and wore a gray suit. Even though the weather outside was bitterly cold, he wore no overcoat. He appeared lean and limber, and carried himself as if getting into fights—and winning them—were part of his lifestyle. The other men looked him up and down, then looked away, as if concluding that his man might take offense at being stared at.

"Where's Chies?" he asked, his voice toneless.

Tuffy Lavagetto, who fancied himself both a funny guy and a tough dude, got up and walked over to the stranger. "Piss off. Chies is busy."

"I'm not going to ask you again." The lack of

anger in his tone made his words that much more chilling.

The two men eyeballed each other, wondering if they would fight, and if so, which man would win. But then Chies, who had been watching the confrontation, said, "Tuffy, sit down."

Tuffy scowled as she nodded and sat.

The stranger and Chies stared at each other for the longest time. Finally the stranger strode across the room to face Chies. He said, "I've come for the job you promised me."

Chies nodded and grinned. He stepped aside from the doorway and gestured for the stranger to go inside. Chies followed.

"Jesus, Francis," the men heard him say, "you sure took a long time to come see me."

Clark took another sip of his cocktail. "This guy Francis was said to want to organize the gambling in Vancouver into a cartel—one big organization divided into smaller ones with rules and regulations. His idea was a new thing to the gamblers here but they were very open to it. So he called a meeting of all the gambling bosses in Vancouver."

If Chies had known what was going to happen, he probably would not have given Francis a job. But he did hire Francis as a runner, which did not last long because Francis was far too intelligent and ambitious to be content with such humble employment. A natural organizer, he soon lorded over the other runners.

To everyone else in the business, Francis Stone remained forever a stranger, the guy who walked in and soon became one of Aldo Chies' most valued associates. Only Chies knew who Francis really was, and Chies said nothing.

Francis sat with Chies at the table. The city's gambling interests were well represented in the room; the big bosses had all shown up.

They met in a hotel room, and Chies had chuckled at the sight of all these impeccably dressed heavies marching through the lobby past the gawking desk clerk—did the cops know that these rich, powerful bad guys were having some sort of meeting today? Upstairs, they all had coffee and cigarettes as they scribbled notes on pads that Chies had provided for their convenience. At about two o'clock in the afternoon, as the Vancouver sun streamed into the room, Chies got up and began to speak.

"You know why you have been asked to attend this meeting, but I will remind you anyway. There are rumors flying around that the premier has appointed a special prosecutor to do away with men like us. If a guy comes in and we can't control him in some way, we're fucked. So we must deal with this matter immediately." His voice was businesslike yet conversational. He was simply one businessman speaking to his peers and attempting to persuade them to see things his way and protect their professional interests. The fact that he was asking them to let him be the boss of bosses did not matter much. When Francis had first suggested that Chies handle their predicament in such a fashion, Chies had laughed. But Francis then explained things so eloquently, and in such detail, that Chies began to nod in agreement, especially as public outrage over local gangsters intensified.

"Under this plan we've worked out," Chies was

saying, "we would be able to do business without interference from the police. We can reconcile our differences by consulting a commissioner—our own commish, appointed by us. No more shootings, no more publicity, no more bullshit threatening our livelihood.

"There's plenty of money in it—more than enough for each of us if we're smart. Up till now I think sometimes that we haven't been smart, but now it's time to get smart. We're a huge business and, if we're going to stay big and powerful, we have to deal with trouble as soon as it happens. We need to protect our investment." He sat down.

The first guy to stand up was Moore from New Westminster. "It sounds very nice, but who will make a guy stay in his territory if he wants to expand?"

"The commissioner," said Chies.

"And how would he do that?"

"By meeting with the parties involved."

"And if that didn't work...?"

"It *would* work," said Chies.

Moore rolled his eyes. Chies sighed at the lameness of his own answer.

Francis Stone got up. "It *would* work," he said, echoing Chies. "We would make it work. We would appoint a commissioner and make it work for everyone's benefit."

Moore said, "This commissioner—who would he be, anyway? One of us?"

Chies grinned, knowing that Stone would urge them to make Aldo their commissioner. "The commish," Stone said, "would be...me."

Chies jumped up and cried out. "You? Who the *fuck* do you think you are?"

Stone stared at him for a few moments.

Moses Solomon, the old man who ran gambling in East Vancouver, shook his head. "We haven't even *started* this new organization yet and already we're screaming at each other about who gets to be the commissioner."

"I'm the only guy here without his own territory," said Stone, "so I'm the disinterested party and the logical choice. I don't give a shit who gets what for the simple reason that it's *yours*, not *mine*. If we don't have a cartel and a commissioner, the Crown's special prosecutor will turn us against each other and we'll basically self-destruct—and I guarantee you that's what he has in mind."

Chies sat back and thought, *Damn! He's right! Maybe he should be the commissioner. I can control him and he can control the cartel.*

"Let's just go ahead and make him our commissioner right now," said Chies.

"How much would it cost us to do things Stone's way?" asked Moore.

Yeah! thought Francis. *They're letting me have my own way without a fight.*

"So," asked Moore, "what's the damage? How much will this new arrangement cost us?"

"It depends," Francis said, "on how much business each person does." He reached into his pocket and pulled out some envelopes. "Each of you gets one of these. It provides all the details you'll need." He handed them out.

The men opened their envelopes and read the documents with intense interest. Francis supposed they disliked much of the messages' contents.

Solomon said, "I can live with this."

Moore said, "Bullshit. I won't be havin' anyone

tell me what I can and can't do."

"In front of you are a pad and pencil. If you don't like what's in the envelope, write N on the pad, sign it and pass it to me."

Presently Francis said, "The only N is from Moore—"

"Because it's bullshit—" blurted Moore.

"But we're going to do it. You don't like it? Leave the room."

Scowling, Moore struggled to his feet and bounded out of the room.

The other men looked at Stone, paying close attention to how he handled that situation. They needed to have some clue as to how he would deal with the inevitable future conflicts that arose from this cartel he seemed so eager to form.

Francis walked over to the far end of the room and picked up the telephone that sat on a table. He said, "Moore wouldn't go for it." Click.

Stone went back to his own seat and sat down. "O.K., let's do this thing. We'll need somewhere to call headquarters and I have just the place. It's in the West End..."

Shit, Chies thought. *He's got it all figured out.*

"People had trouble believing what I've just told you," Clark said to Amnon, watching the man's face to see some trace of surprise there. He found none.

"The cops said it was ludicrous that Bradley Moore was whacked by a brand-new cartel comprising the gambling kingpins of the city.

"After the killing of Moore things got quiet and everyone—the cops, the media and the public—got bored and paid attention to other things. There seemed no need for that 'special prosecutor' who appeared to be so crucial not long before.

"Therefore, organized crime in Vancouver pretty much belonged to Francis Stone. He set up an office in the West End called Francis Stone Enterprises that served as the nerve enter for all illicit activities in our city. All the way from here to Toronto to New York to Miami to Los Angeles, if you were in the Mob and you wanted to expand into Vancouver, you had to get Francis Stone's approval. Everyone knew that.

"By late Nineteen-forty Francis Stone Enterprises

had grown to occupy four floors of one Vancouver skyscraper. Francis had it all organized as one efficient, squared-away, no-bullshit business.

"He retained the best law firm in downtown Vancouver. They said, 'Francis, we know your game, what you're about, and we're going to show you how to launder your dirty money in the safest, most discreet manner possible.' And they did exactly that.

"Later on the press would go crazy with, 'Let's get Francis Stone' and, 'The special prosecutor assigned to fight organized crime in Vancouver is Clark Ruttledge.' But I couldn't get anything on Francis so I actually made an appointment to see him in person.

"I dialed his number and asked for him. I got as far as his secretary. She asked, 'May I ask who's calling?' and I said, 'Clark Rutledge.'" He laughed. "Well, you could hear the panic in her voice. She sure as hell knew who *I* was! And I was calling to speak to their Number One Man!

"So she put me through to him. Got on and said, 'Stone speaking,' just cold and businesslike as all hell."

Clark took a deep breath and looked at his drink. He set it down, got up and walked over to where Tina and Amnon sat. He stretched his back and looked down at his wife, who said, "This is the first time I've heard this story." He nodded and went on.

"I said, 'This is Clark Rutledge.' He understood the context of my call—'I'm your lifelong pal Clark and my job now is to throw your ass in prison'—but it didn't faze him one bit. He just said, 'I know.'"

"I said, 'I'm Clark from way back. We used to hang out together. Remember?'?

"He said, 'I remember.'"

"I said, 'I want to talk.'"

"He said, 'So talk.'"

"I said, 'You need to find a new business. You have no idea how much danger you're in. Everyone is after your ass.'"

"'That right, eh?' he said.

"'Francis,' I said, 'be serious.'

"'I am serious. I never joke with Crown prosecutors,' he told me.

"'Francis,' I said, 'I'm trying to help you.'

"'Then help me by minding your own freakin' business,' he said.

"'O.K., if that's the way you want it,' I said.

"'Anything else I can do for you, Mr. Rutledge?' he asked me.

"I sighed and said, 'No, nothing. I was just remembering way back when, years ago, when we were kids. Amnon, you and I used to hang out together—'

"'That was then and this is now,' he told me. Then he hung up the phone. I sat there for the longest time, knowing that he had things set up so that I would never be able to charge him with anything."

Tina said, "What would you do for Francis if you could?"

He shook his head. "But he's dead."

"What if I told you he was still alive?"

PART SIX

Chapter 1

Chies sat waiting in my office when I got in. He jumped up and said, "The heat really is on, Francis."

"I can tell that you're nervous."

"They're after me because they figure they can't get to you."

I smiled. I paid good money to a guy in the premier's office so that he would tell me about the premier's war on racketeering.

"We must do something, Francis. Our associates are getting worried that the Man might try to put us all out of business."

"Good luck with that." I laughed. Aldo and the rest of them talked tough and truly seemed to consider themselves bad dudes, but whenever real trouble happened they came running to Uncle Francis.

"Aldo," I said, "what do you want me to do or say?"

"I want you to get to Clark Rutledge and tell him to lighten up on us."

"I told you that I tried that and it didn't work," I lied. I had no difficulty when it came to lying to Aldo Chies. I was only too happy telling him whatever I wanted him to know or think. But I knew that Clark Rutledge was too smart and savvy to believe even the most convincing bullshit.

"Can't you find any dirt under his nails and blackmail him into ignoring us?"

"Nope."

"How about his family?"

"His father is the grand old man of Vancouver politics. No scandals, no nothing."

"His old lady?"

I shook my head. "The only dick she rides is her old man's."

Aldo let out a huge sigh. "There must be some way of stopping him."

I got up and walked over to him. "Oh, there is: I walk into his office and say, 'O.K., Steve, here I am.

What can I do for you?"'

Aldo winced. "You know I don't mean that."

"Do I? Do I know that? I'll tell you what I do know—I know that you and your guys come crying to me each time the tiniest thing goes wrong. We are involved in an illegal enterprise, which means that something will always go wrong. The Man has one job: To lean on us till we bend or break and 'fess up about our business so they can bust us and lock us up.

"So my advice is: Be cool, shut the fuck up and let me make the big decisions. I'm sick of having you guys crybabying and bellyaching whenever things don't quite work out.

"The way I see it is this—you and yours have put me in this job to look after things and that's what I'm doing. You want the job?"

Aldo threw up his hands. "Keep it, Francis."

I knew that Aldo and his associates had private talks about me and how much value I deserved.

"Go back to your associates and tell them to man up. Tell them to accept that I'm the boss and they need to do as I say.

366

"I've made arrangements so that if a gangster gets busted, I'll have him released immediately. You tell them it's business as usual until I say otherwise. Understand?" I went back around and took my seat.

Aldo got up and started for the door. "I'll tell them, Francis." Then he left. I got the feeling our conversation had gone not quite as he had planned it.

I got on the phone and said, "Get me Fallon." He was the top crook at the big Vancouver law firm. I needed to tell him to tart working on setting up a service to bail out the gangsters as soon as they were arrested. Fallon could do that easily enough and those gangsters, once busted, would be released immediately and therefore know that Uncle Francis is in charge, taking care of business and making sure that jail terms expire after fifteen minutes. Another thing that concerned me was that most of my associates were blabbermouths and cowards who, if entrusted with confidential information, would, the moment they got busted, start snitching us off in exchange for the lightest possible sentence. No, better just to have my lawyer spring them out of jail before they were interrogated by the coppers.

As soon as I got off the phone with Fallon, I sat back and took a breath. I had many things to do, and I do mean that *I* had to do those things, if I wanted those things done right.

Chapter 2

I sat at my desk forever, daydreaming, spacing out. Maureen had come in, turned on the lights and left. Time went by; I couldn't have cared less. I had really gotten my shit together in the past few years. All the things I wanted—money, quality clothes, gourmet meals—were now mine. If I didn't have a woman, well, I could get every kind of pussy easily enough.

Did I have friends? Probably not. But friends and success were mutually exclusive; you could have one or the other but not both. Also, friends were no substitute for success. Friends wanted you to share your goodies with them, and I wasn't too keen on sharing.

I looked out the window and saw the twinkling lights of Vancouver. I got up and just stood at the window, staring for the longest time at the city lights.

I felt very vain of my status as a native Vancouverite; so many of the people here had come from somewhere else. Well, too bloody bad for them.

Yael had to come and see me just when she did. Bad timing! I wondered about that. Had Clark really sent her? I found out soon enough that when you were involved in an illegal enterprise you couldn't afford to make mistakes. There was no such thing in my business as a small mistake.

I shook my head and sighed. If Clark hadn't gotten that job, things would have been different.

My telephone rang. I picked it up. Allman said, "I have the report you requested."

My watch said ten in the morning, later than I thought. I pictured Stanley Park in my mind and wished I could skip out and go hang out there for the rest of the day. "Come into my office,:" I said.

Presently Allman stood in my doorway. "You wanted to see me?"

"Sit down."

He did as told. "Yessir?"

"Call me Francis. Everyone else does."

He nodded. "My name's Gregory—Greg."

"You don't like this job very much, do you? I mean, you have a couple of degrees from U.B.C., and now you've sunk to working at a place like this, for a guy like me. Too bad for you, eh?"

He shrugged. "A guy has to eat."

I smirked. "Good answer."

"I came to work here because I wanted something different," he said.

"This is illegal," I told him, "but it's still a business." Then, "How much am I paying you?"

He named the number.

"What would you say if I doubled your salary?"

"I'd thank you."

"What would you do for that raise?"

"What would you want?"

"Well, if I found out that Ministry of Justice wanted to find out what I was up to and they sent someone to work for me and spy on me and I wanted to give the authorities inaccurate information about me, would you help me with that?"

He blanched and swallowed hard. "So you know I'm the one who's been spying on you?"

"Yeah. I knew you were one of them when I

hired you."

"Why did you hire me?"

"Because I needed an extra pair of hands. Don't worry—I'm not going to have you whacked. I don't run my business that way."

He sat back in the chair and nodded.

"You've been here eight months. In that time you have learned nothing about my organization that you could use against me in a court of law. My financial interests are many and varied, but if you think you can build a case against me, forget it."

He offered me a small, sad smile. "I believe you're right."

Actually, I was lying. Much of my business was illegal as all hell and he had come very close to learning what he needed to know to bring me down. But that didn't happen.

"I should go now," he said.

"Why? You've been a good worker. Stick around. Turn in your badge and work for me as a second career. Or moonlight for me. I don't much acre one way or the other."

"I don't think so."

"Then goodbye and good luck."

He got up and left. I went to the window and stared out at downtown Vancouver for the longest time.

Chapter 3

At some point I decided I was the biggest fool in Vancouver for neglecting some of the most important people in my life. I got into my car and reminded myself of the address I knew so well: Yael Lichtmann, 345 Point Grey Road, Vancouver.

Presently I pulled up in front of her building, a majestic white edifice that looked even more imposing on this foggy evening. I went up to the front door, turned the knob, yanked it open and walked into the lobby. Up I went to the fifth floor.

I could hear voices from inside the suite as I rang the doorbell. Yael answered the door and I watched her blanch.

"Why did you come here? How did you get in?" Her voice was just above a whisper.

"I wanted to see you. The door was unlocked."

"Damn security," she muttered. Then, "You must leave. You can't come in. Steve's here."

"You came to see me and wouldn't leave till you saw me, so I'm repaying the favor."

She grabbed my arm. "I repeat—Clark is here. If he sees you, he will have to arrest you.

I smiled. "He won't bust me. He doesn't have the balls for it."

"Oh, he'll do it," she said. "He'll bust your ass and lock you up. You don't think so, but he will."

"I know he won't. Let me come in and say hello to ol' Steve."

She stood inches away. I could smell her delicious perfume and see the rise and fall of her firm, plump breasts as she breathed.

I leaned over and kissed her. I had bussed many, many women in my life, and it seemed that each one kissed in her own unique way. Yael did nothing at first; her lips, smooth but limp, let themselves be kissed by my own. But then she wrapped her arms around my neck and got me into a firm lip lock.

She pried himself away from me and said, her eyes looked full of yearning, "Now, *please* go away."

"You don't mean that. If I leave right now, I want you to come with me."

She looked this way and that, as if believing that the words she sought to speak to me were written on the walls to her left and right. "O.K.," she said at last. "I'll go with you. Let me tell the others that I'm stepping out. You go wait in your car."

"I'll wait right here."

Yael shrugged and disappeared into her living room. Soon she came back out with her coat draped over her arm.

"May I help you with that?" I asked her.

"Let's just get out of here. I'll put it on while we're outside."

Back on the street, she said, "Is this your car?"

"One of them."

"It's not much."

"It gets me where I need to go."

"And where might that be?"

"The Hotel Vancouver. I've moved there for the time being."

"Well, aren't you the lucky one?"

"I suppose." I grabbed her again and tried to

kiss her but she pushed me away.

"Is that why you brought me here?" she asked, wiping her mouth. "I'm leaving." She headed for the door.

I grabbed her by the shoulders and said, "If I hadn't wanted to see you so badly, I wouldn't have gone out all the way to Point Grey."

"You should just come out and say what you feel," she told me, "instead of keeping it all inside and trying to play head games with people all the time." Then she threw her arms around me and kissed me for what seemed like hours. "I love you. I've loved you all my life. I couldn't imagine loving anyone else the way I love you."

I held her in my arms. I believed every word she had just said. I supposed I already knew what she had told me—I had known it for years.

The telephone rang. Room service. "Mr. Stone, you wanted something?"

"Cold chicken and a bottle of champagne." I hung up. To Yael I said, "Now, take off your coat, please."

She nodded. Her face had a rosy hue from the

brisk air. Underneath her coat she wore a simple black evening dress. "You checking me out?" she asked with a fake snarl.

"Damn straight," I retorted.

We sat on the sofa and I buried my face in her hair. Then for myriad long moments we looked into each other's eyes. Her eyes asked, *Do you love me?* My eyes answered, *You know I do.*

She murmured, "Maybe this is a dream. I'm afraid I'll wake up and you'll be gone."

I said, "This is no dream."

Yael sighed and smiled. She rested her head on my shoulder and I smiled, too, knowing that I was safe at home with the woman I loved.

Chapter 4

I heard a soft knock on the door. "Come in," I called out, too lazy to get out of bed and let him in.

The room service waiter wheeled a tea cart into the middle of the room. "Good morning, sir. Shall I serve?"

"We're fine, thanks," I told him.

He bowed and left the room. We climbed out of bed, put on robes and Yael put some chicken on my plate while I uncorked and poured the wine. I was famished so I devoured my food. Yael watched me. She said, "You haven't changed, gobbling up your food like that. You did that when we were kids."

"I was a growing boy. I still am," I said as I swallowed a mouthful of food.

Presently we were both finished. We snuggled on the sofa as some soft music played on the radio.

Ordinarily I liked rock music but this sweet stuff sounded O.K. I liked the fancy furniture that filled this suite; the expensive stuff always seemed more comfy than the cheap stuff.

"Why did you pretend in the hospital that you didn't know me?" she asked now.

"Because I hated to have you know that I was in rough shape."

"Yeah, that was a difficult time for you."

"Worse than you could ever imagine."

"Did you ever manage to reconnect with your aunt and uncle?"

"Nope. Couldn't find them."

"That's a shame. I know how many times I feared never seeing you again. I was afraid of waiting for you and becoming an old maid."

"There must have been other guys."

"There were, but none of them was Francis Stone."

"I'll never leave you," I said simply.

"I'm not afraid of that," she told me. "I know that Clark knows about your business and he's trying to send you to prison forever. Lots of people want to see you dead or in prison. It scares me."

I chuckled. "No big deal, baby. They've got nothing on me that will hold up in court."

"But it's real, isn't it? Clark isn't kidding when he says he can bring you down."

"Clark can try," I said with a shrug.

"We couldn't get married if there was a chance you would go to prison."

Who said anything about getting married? I thought. But then it occurred to me that she would be fun to come home to. We could get something worked out. We *had* to.

Chapter 5

I awoke to the peal of my telephone's bell. I'd had my worst night in years—I couldn't sleep, tossed and turned all night, and around dawn I lapsed into a restless half-sleep. I picked up the receiver and said, "What you want?"

"Francis." I recognized the voice—Jay Fallon.

"Jay, what you want?"

"I've been trying to reach you at the office but you hadn't gotten in yet." I looked at my clock and it said eleven-thirty. "They busted Marco Rigoni this morning," he told me.

"Well, bail his ass out. That's why I'm paying you the big bucks."

"Francis," he said with an audible sigh, "this is a different kind of thing—it's a morals charge. He took a couple of underage girls up to his place out of town. The newspapers are loving it. The kids' are outraged about it and the RCMP won't let me talk to him till their investigation is complete. As you know, the Mounties take forever to do things."

Shit!

"Get to the kids' parents and pay them off." I didn't want Rigoni to be in police custody for long; he might be the kind who, if they leaned on him a little, would snitch us all off.

"It's not that simple. This is a federal charge; it's out of the kids' parents' hands."

"I don't want to hear any excuses. Just do whatever is necessary to get Rigoni out of prison."

Click.

I got to the office at around noon and sent for Fallon. He came quickly enough; he wiped sweat from his forehead.

"Give me some good news," I said.

He shrugged. "These things take time."

"Well, as soon as you get him out of jail, get back to me with that good news."

He nodded and hurried out of my office. Next I told Maureen to get me Al Sullings.

"Sullings," I said, "this is Stone. I need to see you tout de suite."

"No can do," he replied. "I refuse to have anything more to do with it."

Click.

I called Paul Josephs and told him to come see me right away

Chapter 6

The next morning Fallon got Smits and Matalin released from jail. Later in the afternoon the judge allowed Rigoni to post bail, and I announced that I wanted all of my associates to attend a meeting in my office at eight that night. Fallon couldn't get to the kids' parents with my deal, so I called him and said, "Fuck it."

The day went well. The pool increased by about thirty thousand dollars despite the handicaps intended to keep it down, which resulted in a net loss of only twenty. Cops were still arresting runners on the street and Hizzoner was trying to get the telephone company to terminate service to bookies' offices; but bookmaking and gambling, albeit illegal, were also popular and often profitable. The mayor made it clear that he wanted to cut the bookies' telephone lines, but his order was kicked around forever and finally lost somewhere under someone's desk.

Fallon came in to see me late in the day and told me what was going on at his end. Rigoni would have to face trial and probably would be convicted. Matalin and Smits would be tried, too, but the cases against them were fairly weak. If they lost, they would probably do only a year or two, if that.

The newspapers loved it. They made a big deal of every word Rutledge said. They put his picture on the front page, and his political career started to look brighter than the July sun. They ran pictures of him entering the courtroom in his dapper dark suit and hat.

I met up with Josephs and he told me that things were going quite well with the behemoth law firm I had sent him to. That firm understood our involvement in illicit activities and our need—or at least desire—to hire them to protect us from the Man. That big law firm told us they would consider representing us and get back to us within a day or two.

I went out to dinner at around seven and returned

to the office not long after eight. Most of my associates were already there and I shook hands with a few of them. I offered them cigars and we all lit up.

I stood before them and began to speak.

"You read the newspapers, so I don't have to tell you what's happening.

"We have a business to protect and certain people out there want to destroy this business that we have worked so hard to build. If we want to defeat our enemies, we need to work together—more so than we have ever worked before.

"We must stand together and not take bullshit from anybody. We have had some bad days lately and will probably have some more bad ones, but then the good ones will return."

Aldo Chies nodded. "I think Francis should make the big decisions and that we should do as he says."

"As you know, a couple of us were busted recently and we don't know yet if they're going to do some serious time. My main concern right now is that the rest of us not be arrested. If you're free, stay that way.

"Those of you who are married need to go home to your wives every night. Stay out of craps games and poker games and gambling joints. I don't want you to be arrested for anything—not even spitting on the sidewalk.

"If you have any pussy on the side, get rid of it. Send the bitch to Florida so she can work on her suntan. You don't need her around here because the cops might start asking her questions and she might start telling them what they want to know."

I looked at Ambueg. "If you find out there's a stolen this or that available for next to nothing, stay away from it." He loved buying and selling hot items. "If any of you has a financial interest in a brothel, get rid of it. The more of you who get busted, the harder it is for the rest of us to do business as usual.

"You guys have an amazingly soft, easy life right now. Time to toughen up and deal with the challenges of running an illegal enterprise."

Chies said, "What happens if *you* get busted?"

"In that case," I replied, "pack up and go home. Game over. This operation cannot survive without me."

"We could survive without you," he said.

I smiled. "You think so, eh? Well, good luck with that." Then, "You guys should all keep your guns in their holsters. You start getting into shootouts with the cops, we're fucked for sure."

Presently our meeting ended. I made sure I told them what was in their own interest rather than mine because they were all selfish bastards whose worldview was just ME ME ME ME ME.

Well, I said to myself, if they think they can do business without me, let 'em try. Let them just fuckin' try.

Chapter 7

I entered my apartment at about eleven o'clock. A couple of days had passed since Yael had been here, but I could still feel her presence. I got made and cursed aloud. I felt I was getting old and soft when a woman could do such a thing to me. I had never let any female get to me since Anne Marie, and I was damned if I would let that happen now.

I turned on the radio and listened to some music. Then the telephone rang. The desk clerk said, "A Mr. Sullings is here to see you."

"O.K., send him up."

Presently he arrived. "Hello, Sullings," I said.

"I'm here on official business, Mr. Stone, he told me.

I crossed to the sofa, gestured at a chair for him, and offered him a drink. He declined, so I poured one just for myself. "So, what's on your mind?"

He sat and eyeballed me for a moment. Then he spoke, and, with great care, said, "I've worked for you for about eight months."

I nodded.

"I know perfectly well what your business is, but there are a few things I would like to know just for personal reasons. Sharing what you know may benefit you as well."

I shrugged. "Ask away." I swallowed a mouthful of my cocktail and wondered what he would ask me.

He leaned forward. "Do you have any connection with the gangsters in Toronto, Montreal or New York?"

"No," I answered, telling him the truth. The gangsters in those cities did their thing and I did mine.

"The general opinion is different from what you've just said."

I smiled. "I can't help what others think or say."

"How about other activities?"

"You mean drugs, prostitution and usury Not me. Others do those things but I don't."

"So your only thing is gambling?"

"In one form or another. I see my business as moving money around, much like Howe Street, Bay Street or Wall Street."

"How long have you known Yael Lichtmann?"

His question surprised me. "For quite a while."

"She seems to speak highly of you."

"And I her."

"Why did she come by to visit you the other day?"

"She's a social worker. I guess she wanted to try to help me help myself."

"About six years ago at Vancouver Centennial Hospital. I was ill. I was walking down the street, talking nonsense to myself. I ended up hospitalized for psychiatric illness caused by malnutrition. I had been unemployed for some time, sleeping on the street or in public washrooms, and I guess she felt sorry for me."

"Sounds like you had quite a time of it."

"You can't imagine." I smiled; Yael hadn't snitched me off.

He nodded. "I've got to get back to work." As he was leaving, he said, "You know, Mr. Stone, you could be just as successful in another, legitimate enterprise."

"Could be. But this one gave me my chance."

"You could go legit and not have to face racketeering charges and incarceration."

He then left and I called Yael. A man answered—Amnon.

"Is Yael available?" I asked.

"Not right now. May I take a message?"

"No, I'll try again later."

Pause. "Francis, is that you? This is Amnon. How's it goin', eh?"

"The pigs are hassling me."

"You mean Steve? Don't take it so seriously. We've been friends all our lives."

"Well, this cop just came by. He said, 'The other day I spoke to a lady named Yael Lichtmann and she said things about you...' I'd like to ask Yael about that visit."

When Yael got in, she called me. "I understand you phoned earlier."

"Yeah, I found out that Special Agent Sullings spoke to you. I wondered what he wanted."

"You mean you wondered what I told him."

"Yeah."

"I told him what he already knew." Then, "You don't trust anyone much, do you?"

"Not much." I added, "Since you didn't snitch me off, I'll send you a dozen white roses in the morning."

"Don't bother. I don't need your largesse."

Click.

I smiled as I hung up the phone. She would come around. She would fall in love with me and spend her life with me, if that was what I wanted.

Chapter 8

This was Christmas Eve Day, and as I sat in my office I could hear the thump-thump-thump of music from other parts of the building. Soon I would have to leave my office and join the party, to put in a personal appearance that reminded everyone that Francis Stone, the boss of bosses, was not just a myth or rumor but a real live person. Most of our employees never saw me because I used a private entrance. I mostly left the management of each department to its head. What was happening on a day-to-day basis throughout the organization reached me through my top executives.

Maureen came in wearing a new dress. At these parties the ladies often did that—wore new dresses, had their hair done, prettied themselves up, flashed big bright smiles. "If you don't need me anything else," she said to me, "I would like to go home now."

"I'll survive," I told her.

I went out and joined the party. The music blared and the employees danced and ate and giggled. Ordinarily I felt powerful and admired at such functions, but at this one I felt lonely and anything but merry. I decided to leave.

"Mr. Stone?"

I turned around and saw a young lady who looked scarcely old enough to buy a cocktail.

"Would you care to dance?" she asked.

"Let's."

People's mouths dropped as I led her to the floor. *Well, let them gawk*, I thought. *It's my floor and my party and my company.* This was the first time I had ever danced at one of these functions.

"What is your name?" I asked.

"Lynn Lamb," she said.

Something about her told me that she was far too young and sweet and innocent to be working for me. Gambling, like drugs and prostitution, was a dirty business, and I hated to see a fresh young thing like her in any way connected with it. I told myself to ask

Maureen to find out which department Lynn worked in and have her fired.

Chapter 9

I went mute. My stomach felt queasy and for a moment I thought I would vomit, but I just swallowed hard and stood there.

"Search him," said one gunman to the other.

"Don't have to," said Lynn. "He's clean."

"Search him anyway. We don't take chances with Francis Stone."

I stood there as they searched me. Then I looked at the woman as she stood by the man with the gun. She looked composed, even complacent. I tried to figure them out and understand who they were and what they wanted of me.

"Turn around," one of them told me, "and go back out to your car."

I nodded and did as told. It's always best to cooperate with the other guy if he has a gun and you don't.

Once inside my car, I told myself that two people from my past—Clark and Aldo—were also probably going to be in my future. Clark wouldn't do me like this—he just wouldn't—and Aldo, if he was out to get me, would have wasted me by now.

"Back to Vancouver," said the gunman to the woman as she got behind the wheel. To me, he said, "You're going to go see your pal the Crown prosecutor."

I let out a little sigh of relief. At least they weren't going to kill me. But I still couldn't figure out why Clark was handling this matter this way. I said to the woman driving the car, "You're making a fool of me."

"It's been easy enough to do," she replied.

I nodded; I had made her work a real no-brainer.

"How long have you been down at my place?" I asked her.

"I didn't go except that once. I just went in and waited for you—"

"Shut up!" yelled one of the gunmen.

We did as told.

By and by we reached downtown Vancouver.

406

"Go to the Madison Hotel," said the gunman.

I knew the place, a fancy joint on upper Granville Street. Things were starting to get interesting; the Madison was a place where shit happened and big money changed hands.

We parked the car and got out. We headed for the lobby. The gunman told us to have a drink at the bar because we were early.

Soon I stood at the registration desk, checking in. Oh, I thought, they are going to frame me for something.

Up in my room, the gunman dialed Clark Rutledge's number and said, "Mr. Stone is here in Vancouver and wants to speak to you here at the Madison Hotel."

Soon he said to Lynn, "It's a done deal. He'll be here soon. You can go tell the boss."

She left and one gunman said to the other, "Go down to the lobby and call me as soon as you see him."

Soon it was him and me, alone. "How much are you getting for this gig?" I asked him.

Silence.

"I'll pay you twice that amount to let me go."

"Not interested," he muttered.

I sighed. Now I understand: Kill Rutledge as soon as he arrives, knock me out cold, put the murder weapon in my hands and make it look as if I had whacked Steve.

I knew Chies was the guy behind this.

Suddenly, I heard knocking at the door as the telephone rang. I answered the phone while the gunman answered the door. The voice in my ear said, "Turk! The place is full of plainclothes pigs!" I slammed down the phone immediately, delighted that Clark Rutledge had arrived with a bunch of police officers.

The door opened and Clark stepped in with a half-dozen guys wearing cheap sportscoats and ties.

"Hey, Francis," he said, "just thought I would bring a few of my best friends."

Chapter 10

As we all stood in my room at the Madison, I said, "Am I under arrest?"

"Not yet. I understood that you wanted a meeting with me."

I shook my head. "Not me. That guy with the gun wanted you to come here alone. Not sure what he had in mind."

One of Steve's cops disarmed the gunman, handcuffed him and took him away. Soon the room contained Clark and me only.

"It was a frameup," I said. "They were going to do you and pin it on me. Looked good on paper"

"Any idea whose idea it was?"

I smiled. "You know who."

I looked at him for the longest time. We had known each other since childhood, and he'd always had a mischievous sparkle in his eyes and a natural smirk. Now he was a man in every way, with a mustache and small paunch. A very serious, no-bullshit man. I missed the kid he had once been.

He looked me up and down. He guffawed. "Shit, you've gotten old!"

"That makes two of us, eh?"

Clark shrugged. "We grew up together...you went one way and I went the other...I didn't think we would meet up again as foes."

"Friendly foes," I retorted.

"As your friend, I would like to look the other way, but I can't."

"No one's asking you to."

He nodded. "I have some questions to ask you." He pulled out a sheet of notepaper.. "Do you know someone named 'Tubby' Kerluke?"

"Yeah."

"How? Where?"

"Around town. Didn't know him; didn't have much use for him."

"And yet, when he opposed your efforts at organizing the gamblers into one pool, you had him killed. Isn't that so?"

I shook my head. "I had nothing to do with his death, and if this is what you have in mind for conversation, it won't work. I wouldn't tell you even if I did know what you wanted to hear."

He frowned. "So you aren't going to cooperate with me."

Clark was a fool if he thought I had any other options. No way in hell would I snitch off anyone to him just because he and I were old friends.

"Here's the deal," Rutledge said through clenched teeth. "I'm doing my damnedest to give you a break because we were boys together. Remember what I said to you? I said, 'Get out of the rackets; get out of organized crime.' Well, you did no such thing, so now I'm going to get you."

You're full of shit! I thought. *If you didn't get me, it was because you couldn't. You haven't done anything for me and you haven't done anything to me because you can't.* I stood up. "Whatever you say, guy."

"I'm going to make you do time," said with a scowl.

"Catch me if you can."

His face turned red. "You lying, thieving, cheating sack of shit."

I smirked. "That's the most intelligent thing you've said all day."

He closed his eyes and took a deep breath. "Francis, I'm sorry. I shouldn't have said that. We go so far back, and I hate to do this to a true friend. But I have a job to do."

"No apology is necessary. You have your job to do and I have mine."

"Francis, why don't you just get out of organized crime?"

Our conversation was on the record. No way in hell was I going to confirm that I was involved in illicit activities.

"I could bust you," Clark said. "Put you in prison for a few years. Give you a chance at a new life after your made parole."

I chuckled. "Are you trying to save me from the people of Vancouver or save them from me?"

Clark smiled. "Very clever."

I smiled back. "I have my moments. Look, Steve, you have a job to so, so just do it. You don't owe me damn thing."

He stood up and held out his hand. "We could be friends."

I shook it. "I thought we already were." Then, "That is a personally thing. This is business, which is quite another."

He kept pumping my hand. "I'm going to bust up your gambling empire."

"Shoot your best shot, baby," I retorted.

He stopped shaking my hand. "Don't think I can do it, eh?"

"Oh, I'm sure you're going to try."

"Will you come down to my office on Monday if I let you go right now?"

"O.K."

Back in my car, I drove along until I heard a voice from the back seat. "Hello, Francis."

"Yael? How did you get here?"

"I have my ways."

I drove out to Aldo's and said, "I have to see a guy about some stuff."

I went inside. Aldo was sipping a cocktail as he supervised a card game. He said to me, "Francis!

What are you doing here? In Vancouver, I mean."

"Let's go into the other room, Aldo. I want to talk to you."

In the bedroom, he said, "Talk."

"Someone tried to kill the Crown prosecutor tonight and make it look like I did it."

"Who ordered the hit?"

"I thought maybe you could tell me."

"I'll let you know if I hear anything."

I soon left. Back at my car, I said, "I'm back. Did you miss me?"

But she was gone.

Chapter 11

My meeting with Clark at his office turned out to be a joke. Fallon was with me, and every time Rutledge asked a question, my lawyer advised me not to answer it. After a while I just sat there with my mouth shut and knew Clark had nothing on me.

The evening papers tried, convicted and hanged me. They ran a picture of me and wrote, "This is the man the city of Vancouver and province of British Columbia call Public Enemy Number One."

I noticed another item, one about a man and woman who had been discovered fatally shot in a field near the TransCanada Highway. The description of the female fit the woman who had been part of the plot to frame me. Aldo had ordered those killings; as always, he was very prompt about eliminating people who knew more than they should about him.

The main thing was that I could come and go as I pleased. I had promised Clark that I would make myself available to him at all times. I called Yael that night.

"What are you doing on New Year's Eve?" I asked her.

"I'll be busy."

"Well, cancel out. I want to party."

Click.

I smiled as I replaced the receiver. Yael would be mine—not right now, but soon and forever. After all, which woman could resist Francis Stone?

January flew in and out, and then came February. Nothing out of the ordinary had occurred, but that meant very little. My new organization was ready to go, and all I needed was an office for it. I would send out Paul Josephs to do that, but only when it became necessary. Things had settled down and mostly it was just business as usual for me.

Things started roiling again in February, when I got a call from Fallon.

"Francis," he said, his voice shaking, "I can't practice anymore. They've suspended me."

"What? Who? Why?"

"The British Columbia Law Society. They've instituted disbarment proceedings against me." He swallowed a sob.

"So that means you can't practice until you've resolved this matter, eh?"

"Right."

"Do they have much of a case against you?"

"Almost nothing. But they're going to drag it out for as long as possible."

They'll drag it out till they can get something on me and tie it to him, I thought. "Well, get on over here and we'll talk about it."

I lit a cigarette and sighed. The other people out there who concerned themselves with my work—law enforcement and rival gangsters—knew I could not continue taking on new associates. This was the beginning of the end. I'd wondered when this would happen. I called Paul Josephs and asked him to come upstairs.

Two days later Amburg was arrested for

receiving stolen property—a diamond necklace. He was a free man on thirty thousand dollars' bail, but I could get ready to wish him goodbye and good luck. I had to tell my associates that Francis' legal department was closed for the time being. They didn't like hearing that; I didn't enjoy saying it.

The next incident happened when someone tipped off Hogan's wife to the two whores on Davie Street. She marched over to the brothel, caught her man getting much too friendly with one of the chippies and started shooting. She just wounded them, but the cops came by, took her to Vancouver City Jail, and did she ever snitch off her hubby! The coppers probably got more information in half an hour about Hogan's illicit than they had gotten from months of their own investigative work.

At the end of the week I sent Paul Josephs out of town and gave his job to the guy who had served as his assistant. I knew our operation would fold at any time.

The last weekend in February was when the shithouse came crashing down. I had divided Hogan's territory between Matalin and Douglas and Chies.

There was too much tension in the air, and too much regret over the loss of a good thing, and a couple of Chies's goons blew away Douglas one morning.

Chies called me personally to say, "My guys did it, in case you were wondering."

I didn't know what to say. Finally I said, "Who gave the order?"

"I don't know," he replied, in a voice whose tone suggested that it didn't really matter, anyway.

"The cops will be looking for the killers," I said.

"If the killers are caught," he told me, "they'll snitch you off."

"*Me?* They work for *you*!"

"As a way of protecting me, they will pin it on you."

Presently I hung up the phone and called Jack Randall, the closest thing I had to a flack, a PR guy.

"Jake," I said, "I have a story I want you to plant in Chip Davis's column."

"Whatever you want, Francis."

"The item should read, 'A certain downtown hotshot knows more about the Douglas shooting than he wants to admit.'"

"Wow! That's pretty hot stuff. I don't know if Chip will go for it."

"There's a check for a thousand dollars in it for you if you can do me this favor."

"Done." Then, "What's goin' on, Francis?"

"Lots of bad shit." Click. Take that, Aldo.

My item made Chip's Monday column. The item was underworld code for, 'These guys need to be killed. Someone take care of him.' Aldo's two hit men accidentally ran into a car that morning.

Chapter 12

I stood in the washroom, checking myself out in the mirror as I shaved. Feelin' *good*. Some spring warmth had started creeping into the April air and sunlight poured into the window. One thing about us Vancouverites—we don't get much sunshine, so when a sunny day comes along, we enjoy the hell out of it. I started singing a pretty song as I splashed on some aftershave lotion and put on my shirt.

I picked up the phone and dialed downstairs. "I'm very hungry," I told the operator, who knew what to send me up for breakfast. Said, "Mr. Stone, two people are here to see you—Dr. Lichtmann and his sister."

"Send them up—and you better make that breakfast for three." Click.

Presently I heard a knock on my door and opened it. There stood Amnon and Yael.

"I've just ordered breakfast for three," I told

them.

"You look good, Francis," Amnon said.

"I hear you're moving up in the world," I I said

He shrugged. "I do what I can."

Breakfast arrived and we tucked it away as fast as we could. Then I said, "Do you ever hear anything about Mrs. George?"

"She died."

"That's a shame."

"Yeah. She was one of the teachers who challenged me and leaned on me when she thought I wasn't leaning on myself enough. If it hadn't been for her, I wouldn't have had the ambition to get this far."

I nodded. "Yeah. I remember her well."

"She thought highly of you, too," Amnon said. "You were born smart—intelligent and streetwise—and she could tell you were a winner, someone who would grow up and do big things in this world. I don't know if being a gangster was what she had in mind for you, but..."

I laughed. To Yael, I said, "Shame about her, eh?"

"I think she was the first person who ever understood you, Francis," she replied without humor.

"Well," I said, "it's all in the past."

Amnon opened his mouth to speak but said nothing. We just sat in silence for a few minutes. Finally I said, "Well, it was sure nice of you two to come over."

"It was my idea," said Amnon. "I wanted to come by and say hi. Our hangout sessions ended a long time ago, and Yael wanted—"

"What did Yael want?" I asked.

"Yael wanted," Yael said, "for you two old pals to get together again. You guys are old friends. You have nothing to gain or lose by speaking your minds to each other."

I thought for a moment. "I want friends but not their advice."

Yael said, "Friends are more than just people who listen to you with much empathy, say, 'Yes, I agree with you,' and tell you whatever they know you want to hear. Sometimes they know they must tell you things you clearly do not want to hear."

I turned to her, not really giving a shit that Amnon was sitting there listening to us. "Sweetie, if you love me, why not just keep loving me and stop trying to get me to do things I don't want to do?"

"Francis, it's *because* I love you that I keep trying to get you to take my advice. If I didn't care I would just shut up."

Amnon said to Yael, "So you meant what you said about him and you."

"I always mean what I say," she retorted. Then, "We came over partly because Amnon has something he wants to tell you." She looked at him.

He nodded. "I was in Germany in Nineteen Thirty-five. I saw what happened there—I saw what happens when the gangsters take over."

I frowned. "You mean Hitler? What's he got to do with anything?" Then, "I remember 'Thirty-five. Here in Canada we kept thinking we wouldn't have to go to war—especially when we kept minding our own business."

"Well, what of it?"

"Gangsters don't last. You are a gangster. You won't last, either."

"If you want me," Yael said, "you'll have to get out of your line of work. It's my way or not at all."

Chapter 13

She stared at me as I lit a cigarette. She said, "You don't understand, do you?"

"Then maybe you should explain it to me. If you love me, you shouldn't care very much about the way I earn my living."

"But I do care. In your business you have to be ruthless and cruel and mean. You have to be a bastard all day and then sleep like a baby all night. I don't want to spend the rest of my life with a gangster.

"No—"

Just then I heard a knock on the door. Amnon. I went over and let him in.

He spent a few moments looking at Yael and me. He had a few questions to ask but said nothing because our facial expressions told him most of what he wanted to know. Amnon, as much as anyone I had ever met, knew when to keep his mouth shut. Presently they left and there I was, alone in my apartment.

I sat there for a while, considering Yael's words and feelings about us. I wanted to tell her that she simply could not end a good thing like ours as casually as she might put down a book. I had invested far too much of myself in it just to throw sand on us and walk away.

But the day was over as far as I was concerned. The joy had gone out of it.

The next months were good for me, or at least easy. My associates were doing their jobs as efficiently as possible and Aldo was minding his manners. Business was brisk and I stashed away the cash in big plastic bags and put them where nobody was likely to find them. I knew that these gravy days would not last forever, but while they did I put the money into garbage bags and considered the cash my own.

In late May, something unusual happened, and it came in a way I would have never predicted. My day had been hectic—we had made lots of money and I needed to make decisions on how to make even more—when Maureen buzzed and said that Moses Solomon wanted to see me.

Presently he sat in my office. We shook hands. He said, "Francis, I want to retire."

"Why?"

He shrugged. "It's that I'm getting too old for the hassles and headaches and *tsuris* of this enterprise. I want to call it a career so my wife and I can go off somewhere quiet for our remaining years."

I sat there and regarded him. This was exactly the wrong time for one of my people to take a hike—especially someone as honest and experienced as Solomon—and if I let him resign everyone would think I was getting soft. Still, he was a grown man who had the right to quit if he believed now was the time to do so. I felt sure he would keep his mouth shut about my business and its secrets till the day he died.

"Our associates won't like this one bit," I said.

"Too bad for them."

"They'll think you've gone chickenshit and maybe, if the cops get to you, you'll tell them about the work we do here."

"But *you* know I won't snitch you off. I'm not about that kind of bullshit."

"What about your territory?"

He grinned. "It never was *my* territory. It was yours. You just let me run it for you. You have other guys working for you who are eager to prove to you they can run it. Give them a chance."

"What about your share of the pool?"

"Same answer. It's yours. Put one of your other people on it."

"Where will you go?"

"Down to the States. I have some land in California."

"When do you want to retire?"

"Whenever it's convenient for you to replace me." Then, "Francis, money you can't enjoy is not worth having. I've saved up some here and there. This business we're in? It's *illegal*, Francis, and that's why it's so lucrative. We have the cops trying to shut us down and throw us into the can, plus we have the other criminal organizations trying to take ours away from us. I want to spend my final years enjoying peace and quiet with my wife."

I nodded. "O.K., Solomon. Do what you gotta do."

He said, with a quivering chin, "Thanks."

"I want you to leave Vancouver by the end of the week. Don't speak to anyone. I don't want any of our associates to know about your 'retirement' till I tell them, and I want that conversation to happen after you're gone."

I dialed Jackson, our new guy. "How does the pool stand now?"

"About one-point-one million dollars."

I smiled. "Draw a check payable to Moses Solomon for one hundred ten thousand dollars and sent it to me immediately." Click.

"I don't need the money right away," said Solomon.

"You deserve this," I told him.

Jackson came up with the check. I sent him away, signed the check, handed it to Solomon and he slipped it into his jacket pocket. "Moses," I said, "do not say anything to anyone about this. Go home and pack a couple of suitcases like you're going away for the week. Get into your car and keep driving till you reach your destination. Then I'll personally deal with everything concerning your departure from my business."

We shook hands and I walked him to the door. He said, "Francis, thank you for being a great boss. I hope you retire early. This is a dirty, dirty business you're in, and it can end up only in prison or death. The money is big and so much of it comes in that you can't believe just how much you're pulling in. But the cops and other crooks are after you and they'll get you even if you think they won't."

I laughed. "Don't worry about me, guy. Just have a happy retirement and maybe think of me once in a while."

"I'll do that, Francis."

He left and I started to think about what to do without him and how to make my associates believe I had handled this situation the right way.

Well, I thought, fuck 'em.

Chapter 14

A few days later Aldo visited me in my office. He sat right across from me and said, "I hear Solomon is thinking about calling it a career."

"That right, eh?" I said as I perused some paperwork.

"As a matter of fact, Francis, some people are saying that you are encouraging him to retire."

"Solomon is a grown man. He'll do what he wants to do."

"Some people think you're starting to slip. They think maybe you should retire, too."

"Let them think what they want."

We stayed silent while I continued with my paperwork. Then I looked up at him. "If you've had your say, Aldo, you can bugger off now."

He stood up and glowered at me. "I just think you should know what people out there are saying about you, Francis. I think sometimes you don't pay enough attention to what people are saying."

I looked up at him. "Oh, I know what they're saying, Aldo. I know it before you do. I also know who's saying what and to whom. My advice to you is for you to keep your big bloody yap shut."

Aldo, who had always prided himself on being utterly unflappable—a precious quality for a gangster—let his hatred for me redden his face. But then he regained his composure. He shrugged and sauntered over to the door. "Have it your way, guy," he said on his way out.

I got on the phone and asked Maureen to get Solomon on the line. He wasn't at his club; I said to try his home.

A woman said in a Jewish accent, "Hello?"

"Is Solomon available?"

"He is not."

"This is Francis Stone, and I need to contact him as soon as possible."

"So do I. Are you his wife?"

"Yes, and I'm worried. He always calls when he's away. He said he was going downtown with a couple of associates."

For the longest moment she stood in the doorway looking at me.

I couldn't speak. I wanted to say something really lame, like, "Where's Amnon?" but even that wouldn't come out. All I needed to do was look at her and I got those special, difficult feelings all over again.

She stepped back from the door, still silent.

I entered the apartment. As soon as the door closed, I kissed her.

"Yael," I said, in just above a whisper.

"Why are you here?"

"I wanted to see you." Until I actually said it, I wasn't sure it really was true. Now I knew it was. I kissed her and said, "Yael."

She placed her hands on my shoulders and whispered, "Francis."

"Change your mind, sweetheart."

"No...I can't."

"Yes you can—"

She shook her head. "Francis, we've got to stop. We've been through this before."

"Yael, will you marry me now—later tonight?" I

said in a voice I did not recognize as my own—childlike, wheedling, pleading. Francis Stone didn't normally talk like that.

Yael took several ragged breaths and said, "I want you so…"

"Then marry me."

She gave her head a weak little shake.

"Marry me," I said.

"I want to be with you forever."

"I love you," I said, my voice shaking. I wasn't used to saying such things to people. "I'm going to do the thing you want most—I'm going to make you a June bride."

"You wouldn't lie to me, Francis, would you?" she asked.

"I lie to everyone else every day, but not to you, sweetie."

She swallowed hard. "I still can't believe it. It's too good to be true."

"Believe it, sweetie. Believe every word of it." I kissed her.

I left her at exactly eight-thirty.

Chapter 15

I parked the car a few blocks from the garage and walked the rest of the way. I knew this neighborhood very well; hell, I knew all of Vancouver very well. But this part of town was one I had covered for Stelfox years earlier. At night it became deserted.

The garage, wide and long, had a front door at its center.

Inside, Solomon was the first man to see me. He and others sat playing cards. He threw down three cards.

I stepped forward and said, "I'll finish your hand for you, Solomon."

Solomon looked up, smiling. The other two jumped up. I recognized one of them as the man named Turk, who had brought me into town once to see Aldo. Turk had his gun on the table and reached over to snatch it up, but Solomon got to it first.

"Solomon," I said, "let him have his piece back."

Solomon sighed and handed the gun to Turk, who didn't take it.

"Turk," I said, "don't be shy. Take your piece."

He just stood there.

"Well, tough guy," I said to him, "you're not such a badass without your piece, eh?"

He stood there looking like an idiot. I punched him in the face and he went down in a heap. "Pick him up and put him into a chair," I said to Solomon. When Solomon stared at me like a Down's syndrome child, I yelled, "Do it!"

He did. Once he had Turk more or less in a chair, Solomon looked at me. Turk wasn't unconscious but he couldn't move.

Solomon eyeballed me. He said, "At first I thought it was you, Francis."

"I gave you my word that it wasn't." Then, "Go home. Your wife is worried about you. You two should leave town forever."

"Where will we go? What will we do?"

"That's your problem, not mine."

Chapter 16

I watched as Solomon walked towards the exit. As he stood in the doorway he turned and waved goodbye. I nodded and he walked away.

I took a nice long look at the two hoodlums. Turk was starting to take some interest in things. He looked at me as I looked at him.

"So," I asked, "how long have you been with Chies?"

"Don't know him."

"Then who told you to pick up Duritz?"

"Guy slipped me money and said, 'There he is. Go get him.'"

"You're a liar. Guy like you doesn't do his job that way."

He just shrugged.

"You beat that gun charge," I said.

"My lawyer beat it for me."

We just stared at each other for a while. I'd had enough experience in dealing with people to know that Turk was angry at someone about something and was waiting for an opportunity to share his feelings with someone.

He'd been staring at me. His stare turned into a scowl. He said. "Why did you kill my sister?"

I smiled. He scowled at my smile. Too bad for him, I thought. "I didn't kill your sister. I didn't know she was your sister. You were her brother—you were supposed to be looking out for me. Why did you let her get into such a vulnerable position?"

He just scowled at me some more.

"I did not kill your sister. But I know who did. You know things, I know things. You tell me some things, I'll tell you some."

He frowned. He pursed his lips. "Maybe we can do that."

I leaned forward. "Well, tell me something I don't already know."

He opened his mouth. Just then the front door creaked open and he said nothing. Instead he cocked his head and listened.

I listened too. I drew my gun and hoped I wouldn't have to use it. I could hear the voices: Chies, Jordan and Pratt. They chattered away as they entered the room.

Turk had his face turned to them. The other guy remained in his chair, paralyzed with fear.

Chies didn't see me yet. "Solomon," he said.

"Solomon couldn't make it," I said, stepping into the light with the gun in my hand. "I'm standing in for him."

Aldo said, "Jeez, Francis! I'm glad to see you! I've been trying to find you. Solomon has been trying to elude us."

I offered him a humorless little smile. "Were you going to try to stop him for us?"

"Absolutely."

"And you brought a couple of the boys over to see him in case you couldn't reach me? Is that about right?"

"Completely."

What nonsense! He had the guy since last night, and if he wanted to level, he had plenty of time to do so. I stood there in silence.

He shifted his weight from one foot to the other. His eyes checked out the room.

I just kept eyeballing him. Suddenly I did something I had wanted to do for quite a while. I used my handgun as a bludgeon and struck him across the face with it.

He went down with a whimper, and when he drew his own weapon I kicked it away. Then I walked over to his gun lay, picked it up and put it into my pocket.

I said to Jordan and Pratt, "Why are you guys here? What's the deal?"

Pratt said, "We don't know what's happening, Francis. Aldo just said he had something he wanted us to see."

I nodded. "Sit down. We need to have a little chat."

They sat. I looked down at Aldo, who remained prostrate on the floor. "You sit, too."

He hot up and took a seat.

Turk was standing behind Aldo. I looked at the two of them. "Turk was going to tell me something when you guys came in."

Turk just stood there, mute.

I leaned forward and glowered at him. "I told you I know who killed your sister. Only one person besides you and me knows what happened that night you set me up. That was Chies. I went right up to his place after it happened and told him all about it. He promised to be on the lookout for the bad guy who did it." I added, "Well, now you know who did your sister."

Turk's eyes blazed with rage. He reached down and wrapped his hands around Chies' neck. Then he began to strangle the man.

Aldo grabbed onto Turk's hands and tried to pry them off his neck. Turk's only worked harder and soon Aldo's face turned red, then blue.

"Hold up, Turk," I said. "He's had enough."

Turk just kept on strangling him.

I raised my gun and pointed it at Turk's face. "Stop it."

Turk let go and Chies fell out of his chair, unconscious. We threw some water on him to wake him up and said, "O.K., listen up. I gave Solomon permission to quit. If you want to live to be his age, you'd better not screw around with me. Until you reach his age, you need to remember that I am the boss."

I looked at them and they at me. Silence. I said more. "Now leave and take Aldo with you. Take him to a doctor. He don't look so good."

The punk who had been with Turk was the first out the door. Then the others split. Turk remained.

He stood there watching me.

"You want something with me?" I asked him.

He smiled. Not a friendly smile, but a respectful one. "You're a tough guy," he said.

"The world's full of tough guys," I retorted.

"You're tougher than the rest." Then, "I'm looking for an opportunity."

I gave him back his gun. "I need a guy who keeps his cool when things get hot, a guy who doesn't have nightmares when he sees nasty things on the job."

"I work as a bodyguard for a living," he said. "I follow orders; I don't ask why."

"You're hired."

Chapter 17

The next morning I called Paul Josephs. "Look," I said, "when you told me that stuff yesterday, I was in too much of a huff to pay attention. Tell it to me again."

He did as asked.

I listened. "Sounds good to me. Do you have to be there for a while?"

"I should be. Why? Is there a problem?"

"No, but there's something I want you to do, and I want you to get back here as soon as possible."

"I'll be in on Sunday."

"Good. Come up to the hotel as soon as you get in." Click.

I buzzed Maureen. "Send Turk in."

Turk entered my office. This was his first time here. He looked around and nodded.

"Sit down, guy. How you feeling?"

"Been better, but I'm surviving." Then, "So, what can I do for you?"

"From now on, everyone who wants to see me will have to see you first, at my office or house. I've arranged to give you the room next to my apartment. Even after I've given my consent for someone to come up to see me, they will have to see you first. At the office you will have a desk in Maureen's office. Any questions?"

"Nope."

I sent him away. I felt convinced that Aldo's next move would be to have me killed. I had to be aware of that, and told myself that my options were to make myself inaccessible to Aldo or have him killed, and I didn't want to mess around with hit men. I wanted much more to screw up his life than end it.

I picked up my private telephone and dialed Yael.

"Hello?"

"Hello, sweetness," I said. "I needed to hear your voice."

She laughed. "I wanted to hear yours, too."

Presently we concluded our conversation and

hung up. I started in on my day's work, chuckling and humming.

That evening I drove over to visit her. Turk had to sit shivering in the car during my three-hour visit but did not complain when I finally rejoined him.

On Sunday morning at about eleven Paul Josephs showed up. He made a face when he first saw Turk, but I told Turk to shoo, and when Josephs and I were alone I told him what was going on.

He nodded. "So, what can I do for you?"

"I want to sell out. This thing is going to end pretty soon and I have other things I want to do. Do you think you could alter the books and records for me?"

He frowned for a few moments, then nodded.

"How long would it take?" I asked him.

"A few weeks of around-the-clock work. But we would have to get someone to replace you or it wouldn't look legit."

"That's easy. We'll use Aldo Chies."

"Chies? Why use him? I thought he wanted to have you killed."

"He wants to kill me. But he wants my business,

445

too. He's going to get it, too, but he doesn't know that yet. He also doesn't know that getting my business would be a bad thing for him."

He grimaced. "I won't ask you to explain any of this to me, but I'll do it. When do you want me to start?"

"Right after breakfast."

I dropped him off at the office so he could start to orient himself to the big job I had just given him. Then I drove over to get Yael.

"How about a drive into the Fraser Valley?" I asked her.

She smiled. "Let me get my hat and coat."

I wondered what she would think when she saw Turk. I would have to explain him to her without getting her too worried. We spent a wonderful day out in the boonies, anyway.

We drove and drove and drove until, finally, we reached the Fraser Valley. We ate at the inn and gawked at the mountains and farmland. Then we drove back into Vancouver.

On June tenth Paul walked into my office looking very pleased with himself. I said, "What are you so happy about?"

He rubbed his hands together. "It's a done deal."

I gave him the thumbs up. "Good to know. Now, hop a flight out to the plant and do your thing there. Buy a house for me and have it fully furnished so I can move out there next month."

"But what if I buy and furnish a house and you don't like it?"

"Then too bad for me."

"I've doctored the books. Want to see them?"

"Like I said, I trust you."

He soon left my office and I called Clark Rutledge.

Chapter 18

After my call went through a couple of secretaries, Clark got on the line.

"This is Francis Stone," I told him. "Are you available this afternoon? I want to see you."

"Come over," he said.

"I can't go to your office but I need to see you soon."

"Let's meet somewhere," he said.

"Stanley Park at four o'clock this afternoon. We'll have dinner there. Our meeting will take some time."

"Four sounds good."

I left the office at three. I told Turk to wait for me at my apartment. Then I drove out to meet Steve.

I arrived at Stanley Park just before four. I waited for a few minutes, and at exactly four I saw Clark enter the parking lot in a dark sedan. I rolled down my window and waved at him. He waved back.

We parked our cars and I went over to shake his hand and say hello. "There's a fish-and-chips place over there. We can eat and talk," I said.

We walked over and bought two orders of fish and chips plus a couple of jumbo iced teas. We sat at a nearby bench overlooking the Burrard Inlet. I said, "So I guess you're wondering about this meeting."

He shrugged.

"How badly do you want me, Steve?"

"It's my job to get you."

I smiled. "Wouldn't it be enough just to bust up the racket? I mean, getting me personally wouldn't stop the racket—someone else would take over—but I could make you a deal. I'll set it all up so you can break it down once I've gone. I'll even give you a fall guy, someone infamous who will go to prison and make you look pretty good in the newspapers."

He sipped his iced tea and smiled. I felt as if we were kids again, being sneaky and naughty. "Why do you want to pull out? You're making a fortune and I really don't have anything on you."

I swallowed a mouthful of halibut. "I'm engaged,

and my fiancée dislikes my current occupation."

He chuckled. "Don't tell me that some woman is going to do what the city, provincial and federal courts failed to do."

"Sad but true."

"Good on her. What's her name?"

"Yael."

He swallowed hard. "*Our* Yael? How long have you two been a couple?"

"I've loved her for years."

"I would like to help you—more Yael than you, actually—but I don't know how. I have a job to do, you know."

"Whatever you say. But if you take me down you'll be making your father look bad. His law firm has helped me for years."

Clark frowned. "My dad would never represent you."

"But he has, many times. We have a long history together." Then, "Look, Steve, we've known each other since we were kids—but we are not kids any longer. We're adults, and we are involved in business here—serious business. Let's suppose that at some point you get enough on me to charge me with something, and when that happens someone drags Chip Rutledge's name into it. You want to know what people will say? They'll say, 'It took Clark Rutledge so long to take down Francis Stone because Stone was paying Chip Rutledge to keep his mouth shut.'"

"I could kill you for saying such a thing, you son of a bitch," Clark said through clenched teeth.

"If you did, just remember that homicide is illegal in Canada, just as it is everywhere else." Then, "Finish your food."

We ate in silence. We walked back to our cars. Clark said, "You know, Francis, you haven't changed a bit over the years. But don't think you can get away with your crap all the time. Your luck may run out at some point."

"It's not all luck, pal. You need to be *smart*, too."

Chapter 19

At just before noon the next morning I got a call from Jay Fallon. He sounded happy for once. "Francis," he said, "the Bar dropped its charges against me this morning."

"Terrific!" I said. I had arranged for that with Steve, but Jay didn't need to know. "Get on over here and we'll celebrate with a drink."

I called Turk into my office. I wanted to talk to Aldo Chies, but that guy wouldn't accept my invitation, so I wanted Turk to go collect him.

Jay arrived at my office soon after our phone call. I got up and shook his hand. "Congratulations! I knew you would make out all right."

He shrugged. "I was worried there for a little while. I'm still not sure why they dropped it."

"Sit down and I'll tell you about it."

He sat and I spoke. When I finished, he said, "Do

you think you can get away with it?"

"I can if you'll help me."

"Whatever you need."

"That's what I like to hear." I smiled. "Don't run off; I want you here when Aldo shows up."

Turk brought Aldo in at just after three. Aldo walked over to me and said, "You know, Francis, you didn't have to send him over to collect me. I'm not a little kid. All you had to do was phone and ask me to come by."

"Well, Aldo, I was just doing you the way you would have done me."

He sighed. "Well, you're here and I'm here. Tell me what you want."

I took a deep breath. "You know that when we started this thing I wanted to run it in a strictly legitimate way. You said sure, but lately, well, you've been insisting on doing things your own way. It would have been easier for me just to have you killed, but I don't do things that way. Long story short—I've decided to buy you out."

Aldo grinned, the way he grinned when he wanted to say, "You're acting like you're the boss, when everyone knows *I'm* the boss." He said, "What do you have in mind?"

"I want you to give up your share of the territory and let me run it all," I said in a quiet voice.

"What's in it for me?"

"A hundred thousand dollars."

He frowned. "That's only what's in my share of the pool. I take a quarter million each year out of my territory."

"Yes."

"And the pool pays about two hundred large per year."

"Yes," I repeated.

He pursed his lips. Presently he said, "What if I refuse to sell?"

"I'm hoping that won't happen."

He saw a chair and sat down. He stayed silent for the longest time. I watched him and could practically see the tumblers move in his head as he looked at everything from every possible angle. At last he pointed at me and said, "What if I bought *you* out?"

I shook my head, delighted by his question. "Not gonna happen. I'm here to buy, not sell."

"What if I made you a huge offer?"

"Such as?"

"Three hundred large and a share of the profits?"

I arched an eyebrow. "Really? How much of a share?"

"A half share, payable monthly."

"You're too generous," I said. "I'll have to think about it."

He licked his lips. He was trying right now to get something he had wanted for a long time. "Francis," he said, "this would be ideal for you. You could have whatever you wanted and never work again."

I smiled. Aldo was certainly playing me for a fool. "Sounds good. But how do I know you're serious?"

"I'll have certified checks for you in the morning."

I caved in. "O.K., Aldo, it's yours."

On the next morning, just before noon, Aldo entered my office. Fallon and I were already there.

"Got the paper?" I asked Aldo.

"That's why I'm here." He took out the certified checks and put them on the desk. "Made payable to Jay Fallon for services rendered. Just like you asked."

I looked at them and nodded. I handed them to Jay, who endorsed them and handed them back to me. I summoned Maureen, my receptionist, who came in with the envelope I had asked her to prepare. She left as I slipped the certified checks into the envelope and put it into my jacket pocket.

I said, "Gentlemen, this calls for a drink." I pulled out my bottle of Canadian Comfort and poured three drinks.

Once our glasses were empty I told Jay to take Aldo around and show him the place. They exited the room together.

I called Picard and asked him to come up with the checks I had ordered him to draw up. They were all in order: the pool split up into its component parts as of this date. I signed them and handed them to Maureen to send out. I made sure that everyone was paid off, including Aldo. Then I departed my office via private elevator and headed over to the hotel.

Paul Josephs sat waiting in my apartment. I handed him the envelope containing the checks Aldo had given me. "I guess you know what to do," I said.

"Absolutely." We had figured out that, too. An

account had been opened in each of the banks where Aldo did business. Each of the new accounts bore the name of my new company, and the checks would be properly deposited into each new account. I went back to the office.

An hour later Paul called me. "Everything is copacetic, Francis."

I hung up the phone without saying anything. Then, with some anxiety, I called a private number.

"Clark Rutledge," said the voice at the other end.

"Francis," I said. "It's a done deal." Click.

Presently Aldo and Jay returned to the office. Aldo beamed at me. "Wow! I knew this was big, but I had no idea it was *this* big!"

I laughed. "Yeah, I'd say it was better than O.K. We can get into the operations tomorrow. Let's have a drink right now." I got out my bottle of Canadian Comfort and we drank.

Aldo drained his glass and just couldn't seem to get the smile off his face. He walked around my desk and sat in my chair. He put his feet up on my desk and pointed at the other seat, the one for guests. "Sit," he said to me.

I smiled. Aldo had no clue as to how much trouble he had gotten himself into, but he would find out pretty damn fast. I sat in the guest's seat. Aldo and I smiled at each other, albeit for vastly different reasons.

Just then the door behind me flew open. I didn't have to turn around and look. I knew who it was.

Chapter 20

Aldo jumped to his feet and yelled, "What the hell...!"

I stood up and turned around. Four men stood in my office. Turk, shoved to one side, held up his hands as one of the men pointed a gun at his stomach.

One of the men said to me, "Are you Francis Stone?"

I nodded.

"We have a warrant for your arrest on charges of conspiracy and bribing public officials of the Province of British Columbia. We have a further warrant and subpoena pertaining to the examination of the books of Francis Stone Enterprises."

Fallon said, "Do you have a writ of extradition?"

"Yes," the man said.

"Let me see it."

The man handed some documents to Fallon, who perused them for several moments. He handed them back and said, "Francis, it looks like they have everything they need. You'll have to go with them."

I did as told.

The man went up to Aldo. "Are you Aldo Chies?"

Our trial ended on the last day in June. On that morning Clark entered the courtroom and walked past Aldo and me. We looked up at him; he didn't look at us. His face was as white as chalk as he spoke to the jury.

"Ladies and gentlemen," he said, "this morning we received from the accountants the results from the detailed examination of the books and records of Francis Stone Enterprises. It says, 'We, the examiners of Francis Stone Enterprises, as originally conceived by the defendant Francis Stone, find that this business is a legitimate and honest one insofar as it has been managed by the defendant. We find that the financing of said business by Aldo Chies, and that Francis Stone at no time participated in the criminal financial activities by his financier.

"While Francis Stone was involved in legal business enterprises, Aldo Chies was involved in gambling and bookmaking."

Presently they acquitted me and convicted Aldo.

Fallon asked, "Francis, where are you going?"

"For a drink."

At the bar, I ordered a double Canadian Comfort over ice. As I sipped it, I felt a hand on my shoulder. Standing behind me was Turk.

"Did you beat this thing?" he asked.

"Nothin' to it," I replied, grinning.

"How about Aldo?"

"Busted." Then, "I hate to drink alone. What's your poison?"

He ordered the same as I was having.

"Aldo has a pretty serious beef," he said. "How much time do you think he'll do?"

I shrugged. "About a decade. But this is Canada—he'll do easy time."

The bar was crowded. We had to be careful of what we said. "Aldo is mad at you," Turk said. "He'll want revenge."

"How do you know that?"

"Because I know Aldo."

I nodded. "He has so many contacts. He'll call in as many favors as necessary. I better be careful." I reached into my jacket pocket for money to pay for our drinks. Instead I pulled out a slip of paper that said *You're a dead man.*

I showed it to Turk. He read it and his face bore no expression. I ordered two more drinks. The bartender set them down before us. We drank them down and got two more. "How will you pay for these?" Turk asked me.

"Like this." I tossed a bill on the counter and we walked out.

We stood in the street for a moment. I said, "Fallon will get you the money. Contact him tomorrow."

"I'll do that."

I waved down a passing taxi. It slowed down and cruised to the curb. I got in. "Later, Turk."

"Goodbye, tough guy!"

I sat back as the cab drove off. I knew I would at some point have to deal with Turk, too, but that was for another day. Just then the cabbie said, "Well, it's your dime, so are we just going to go joyriding around Vancouver or do you have a particular destination in mind?"

Chapter 21

I returned to my apartment and changed my clothes. Then I ordered a car and drove back to Vancouver.

On my way I bought a copy of the Vancouver *Times*. The headline screamed "STONE FREED—CHIES GUILTY." Below it ran a black lead line: "Rutledge smashes Mob." A picture of Clark showed him leaving court after the trial, smiling. "Steven Rutledge, racket buster," read the caption.

I chuckled. Those damn newspapers! They probably believed their own bullshit! Their next thing probably would be to announce he was going to become Canada's next prime minister. I tossed the newspaper into a trash receptacle and drove on.

I reached Yael's building, got out of the car and went inside. The goofy elevator boy from last time was still there. He kept staring at me as we rode up to

Yael's floor. I got out and knocked on her door.

After what seemed an hour, she opened the door and stood before me. It was as if we had never met—I felt like some well-dressed charity representative bugging her for money.

"Yael," I said at last, with a hundred feelings in my heart begging for expression but clueless as to what to say next.

She threw herself into my arms. "Francis! Francis!" Her sobs wracked her entire body.

We stepped inside and closed the door. "Yael, don't cry, sweetheart. It's all over."

"Francis, I was sure you had gone forever. I thought you would never come back."

We sat on her sofa and she said, "It's the last day in June, you know."

"I know. That's why I'm here. I told you that you would be a June bride. Get some things packed and we'll get married tonight."

She shook her head. "No, we can't do that. We're not getting married."

"Why not?"

"Because you don't love me." When I opened my

mouth to assure her otherwise, she raised a hand to shush me. "You don't love me. You have decided that it's time to get married, and I'm as good a candidate as anyone else. It's like that deal you struck with Steve. You don't love me, and I'm not sure you know *how* to love."

"Do you love me?"

"I've loved you all my life. More than you'll ever know. A thousand times I've wanted to marry you and have your children. But I've also known that marrying you would have been the biggest mistake of my life."

I grabbed her by the shoulders. "You bitch! Don't you know how much I've done for you? I've thrown away so much because of you! I had a dozen places in Canada and the States I could have gone to and they never would have caught up with me. I didn't have to quit; I did so because of you. If I had been indifferent to you, I could have beat this thing, even though it would have destroyed Steve's career. What I did, I did for you."

I sighed and got up. I headed for the door.

"Francis!" she cried out in a tiny voice.

I turned around. She looked at me and said, "You're crying!"

Yael and I were married an hour later.

What happened later

Amnon suddenly started to sweat and tremble. He sank into a chair and said to Yael, "What do you mean?"

Steve, too, looked at his wife, wanting answers and explanations. He already knew part of it but was ready for the rest. He sat down and wiped his face.

"We all knew Yael was going to have a baby," she said, seating herself so that she faced them. "When we received that little telegram from Francis that Yael had died in childbirth, we just assumed that the child had died, too.

"Amnon, you were overseas, so all we could do was write to you and tell you what had happened. A month later, Clark went over and our lives just seemed to stop for a while.

Dear Tina,

I am writing this letter that I hope you will receive. It is very strange to write a letter you believe will never be delivered, but even stranger to write one that may actually reach its destination. If you get this letter it will mean, quite simply, that I will be dead. Therefore, I would just as soon not write this letter, but I know it's better that I do.

It seems years ago that we stormed Normandy on D-day, but June 6 was just a little while ago. Since that day I have been able to make sense of many things. So many things have happened; there is much I want you to know and there are things I need to ask of you.

One time years ago Amnon compared me to Adolph Hitler. I laughed then, mainly because I really did not understand what he meant. Now I do; I learned it from living with Yael and from being here in Europe. I've learned that one cannot live without regard for society and the common man. The person who lives that way does so without regard for himself.

I began to wonder what made me what I became.

472

Then I realized that it came from living alone. One can live alone with a hundred others if he shares his heart with none. I lived that way for many years until I married Yael.

As you are aware, Yael died in childbirth. You probably do not know that our child survived. We had a son.

I had thought very, very little about having children. Frankly, I did not want any. But Yael said, "I want to have your baby. I want to give you a son. I want to have him for so many reasons. He will be his father all over again. I can keep you close to me, even when you're far away. I can give him—and therefore give you—all the love and care and dreams you, an orphan boy, had to do without.

"Give me your son, my darling, so that I can make you whole again, make you live again." That is what she told me.

When our child was born and she knew she would not live to raise him, she whispered to me, "Don't fail him, Francis. Give him the childhood and dreams you didn't get. Let him indulge in the pleasures of youth and grow into the man he will be capable of becoming. Give him everything I wanted him to have."

I told her I would do exactly that.

But first I had to come home from the military. When it looked as though I might not come home, I fretted over failing to keep my promise to her, so I ask you to help me keep it. Take our son into your home and raise him as your own. Give him your name and all the things I know you can give.

I am a reasonably affluent man. I do not pretend otherwise. My son will never do without the things money can buy...but what he will lack are those things that have no price tags and are priceless. Such are the things you can give him.

Do not let him grow up as I did—sheltered and clothed and fed, yes, but poorer in human qualities than the most destitute of men. Clearly, a person needs more than food, clothing and money; one who has only those things is less than human. To be more than human—to be a *person*—one needs love, kindness and affection.

A person needs people, a family—he needs an anchor. People give him roots in the earth, to be a part of the human family, to teach him the values that truly matter. Those are the values that I learned from Yael.

I took my son to the Orphanage of St. Anthony and handed him over to Brother Lawrence. I have received letters from Brother, and he tells me that my boy is very much like his dad.